GRIZZLY TRAP

GRIZZLY TRAP

Justin D'Ath

A & C Black • London

For my editor Tegan Morrison,
with thanks

Reprinted 2011
First published in the UK in 2011
by A & C Black
Bloomsbury Publishing Plc
50 Bedford Square
London
WC1B 3DP

www.acblack.com

First published in Australia by
Penguin Group (Australia)
A division of Pearson Australia Group Pty Ltd

Text copyright © 2009 Justin D'Ath

ISBN 978-1-4081-2647-9

A CIP catalogue for this book is available from the British Library.

This book is produced using paper that is made from wood grown in
managed, sustainable forests. It is natural, renewable and recyclable.
The logging and manufacturing processes conform to the environmental
regulations of the country of origin.

Printed and bound in Great Britain
by CPI Group (UK) Ltd, Croydon, CR0 4YY

1
ATTACKED BY
A GRIZZLY

'If you get attacked by a grizzly,' E.J. said, 'lie face down on the ground and cover your head.'

'Won't it eat you?' asked Sally.

'Depends how mad it is,' the American cub scout said. 'Sometimes they lose interest if the person plays dead.'

We were on our way to an international cub scout Jamboree in the Rocky Mountains. E.J. and his dad had collected us from the airport in a minibus that belonged to the Bobcat Creek Scout Group. For the rest of us in the vehicle – six Australian cub scouts and their two leaders (Mum and me) – it was our first ever trip to the USA.

'What if it *doesn't* lose interest?' Guy asked.

E.J. paused while his father swung the minibus around a steep hairpin bend. 'Grizzlies hardly ever eat a whole person,' he said. 'But you might lose a hand or an ear, or part of your bottom if he's hungry – grizzlies especially like bottoms.'

'Gross!' said someone down at the back.

Guy was staring wide-eyed into the steep, forested canyon below us, as if every tree concealed a hungry bear. 'Wouldn't it be better just to run away?'

'Only if you're an Olympic sprinter,' E.J. said. 'Grizzlies can run 56 kilometres an hour.'

I looked around the bumping, swaying bus at all the white-faced Australian cub scouts. Even Mum looked nervous, and she was our pack leader – Akela, the wolf.

'I've heard there aren't many wild grizzlies left in the United States,' I said, trying *not* to look nervous. As Akela's helper, my leader name was Baloo – the bear!

'Are you kidding?' laughed E.J. 'Last time they did a count, there were over 100 wild grizzlies in this stretch of the Rockies.'

Normally I get on well with people. Even if something about them annoys me, I make an effort to be friendly.

But E.J. was starting to get under my skin. With all his talk about grizzlies, no one would want to leave the bus when we reached Glass Mountain National Park, much less spend the next five nights in a tent.

'Have you earned your Dunny Badge yet, E.J.?' I asked.

He wrinkled his nose. 'What's a *Dunny* Badge?'

'I'll show you when we get to camp,' I grinned.

It was the last time I would grin for a long, long time.

E.J. was sitting directly behind me. I'd twisted around in my seat to speak to him, so I didn't see what the others saw. But I saw their faces – suddenly everyone's eyes nearly doubled in size.

'*MOOSE!*' cried Guy.

I had never seen a wild moose before, and I didn't see this one. Things happened too fast. There was the shrill blast of the bus's horn and a squeal of brakes, then the world seemed to tip sideways. My seatbelt pulled one way, gravity pulled the other. The pen from my shirt pocket shot up and hit me on the chin. A map book went sliding up the window next to Joel. Two sleeping bags and a bottle of cordial bounced across the ceiling.

Then – *CRUNCH!* – a silver spray of raindrops exploded through the bus.

That's when my brain finally kicked into action.

Those aren't raindrops, said a little voice in my head, *they're bits of glass from a broken window.*

We'd had an accident. A moose had run in front of the bus, and Mr Johnson had swerved to avoid it. But he'd gone off the road. Trees flashed past the windows, then sky, then more trees, then sky again. The bus was tumbling, like a rolling log, down the steep side of the canyon.

I remembered how far it was down to the river. And how the final 50 metres was a vertical rocky cliff.

We were all going to die.

THUMP!

2
D-D-DEAD!

Everything was upside down. I was upside down. Joel beside me was upside down. The bus was upside down. Dust swirled in through the broken windows. Outside, I could see rocks and grass and pine needles. There was a strong smell of raspberries.

'Everyone stay where you are,' came Mum's voice from behind me. She sounded amazingly calm. 'Try not to move, and don't undo your seatbelts. Is anyone hurt?'

Several voices muttered that they were OK. Someone had the hiccups. Someone else was crying softly, trying not to be heard.

'Will, is that you?' asked Mum.

'My arm hurts,' he snivelled.

'All right, love, we'll help you in a moment,' Mum said gently. 'Sam, are you OK?'

I waggled my feet, then tested my arms, wrists, fingers and neck. Everything seemed to be working. But it was hard to be sure because I was dangling upside down. 'I think so.'

'Good. See if you can free yourself from your seatbelt. Be very careful not to fall on your head.'

It wasn't far to fall, anyway – the bus's roof had caved in and my hair brushed against it. Jackknifing my body, I swung my legs down in front of my chest and undid the seatbelt's buckle. It was lucky I was wearing jeans, because I landed knees-first in a bed of crunchy window glass. Other stuff lay scattered around me – hats, cameras, an apple with a bite taken out of it. And a cracked plastic bottle lying in a puddle of red cordial – now I knew where the raspberry smell was coming from.

'Good work, Sam,' Mum said from somewhere beyond my view. 'Now listen up, Gunggari Pack – and you too, E.J. I want everyone to stay exactly where you are until

Baloo helps you down.'

It felt strange being called Baloo. I wasn't really a scout leader – 14 is too young – but when Joel's dad couldn't get time off to come to America, Mum asked me to fill in for him.

'Sam?' Mum said. 'Could you take a look at Will before you help the others?'

Will was clutching his right elbow with his left hand. His lower lip trembled and tears trickled down his upside-down forehead into his hair. When I asked him to unclip his seatbelt while I supported his weight, Will shook his head. 'Can't move my arm,' he whimpered.

I couldn't support his weight *and* undo the belt buckle – I didn't have enough hands – so I freed Guy first. Together, we lifted Will down and helped him out through one of the broken windows.

'How close was that!' Guy muttered, as we settled Will on a gentle grassy slope about five metres uphill from the wreck.

The bus rested upside down against two fir trees. They grew right on the edge of the cliff, where the canyon made its final vertical plunge towards the river far below.

Both trees sloped out over the cliff at a 45-degree angle, and they'd been knocked half out of the ground when the bus rolled into them. A few bent and mangled roots were all that was keeping the trees in place.

I heard a clatter of falling rocks from the other side of the bus. It sounded like a small avalanche. One of the trees tipped a few more centimetres. The bus wobbled.

'It's going to fall over the cliff!' Guy said.

'Shhhh,' I whispered. I didn't want to scare the cubs who were still trapped inside. 'Stay here with Will while I get the others out.'

That was Baloo talking, not me. The real Sam Fox was terrified. I didn't want to go anywhere *near* the bus. It might roll over the edge at any moment, taking everyone with it.

Including Akela.

Why isn't *she* helping? I wondered, scrambling back in through one of the smashed windows.

As soon as I saw her, my question was answered.

'Mum!'

'It isn't as bad as it looks,' she said calmly. 'Head wounds always bleed a lot.'

She wasn't kidding. Even though Mum had pressed a rolled-up sweatshirt to the side of her head, blood was seeping out around the edges and dripping through her hair like tomato sauce.

'I'll get you down,' I said.

'No, Sam. Help the others first.'

'But . . .'

'No buts,' Mum said. 'I'll be all right here for a few more minutes.'

I wondered if we *had* a few more minutes. The bus could fall at any time. But I couldn't tell Mum what the situation was without the rest of the pack hearing. Someone was sure to panic, and all it would take was one sudden movement to tip the bus over the edge.

As quickly as I could, I began evacuating the remaining cubs. It was Sally who had the hiccups, so I got her out first. Then Emma, then Joel, then Matt. I left E.J. until last – not because he irritated me, but because he seemed calmer than the others.

It wasn't until I got to him that I realised my mistake. E.J.'s hands felt clammy, his eyes were unfocused and his teeth chattered.

He wasn't calm, he was in shock.

'It's OK, mate,' I said, struggling to undo his seatbelt. It was twisted the wrong way, so the release button pressed against his stomach and wouldn't open. 'I'll have you out of here in a jiffy.'

E.J.'s out-of-focus eyes seemed to stare right through me. 'D-D-Dad,' he whispered.

Poor kid. He was in a really bad way.

'I'm not your dad,' I corrected him. 'I'm Baloo.'

He shook his head. 'My dad, Mr J-J-Johnson.'

A chill passed through me. I hadn't given a thought to our driver since the accident. Twisting around, I peered under the headrests towards the front of the bus. Holy guacamole! The forward section was completely caved in. All I could see was the back of Mr Johnson's head, jammed sideways against the crumpled ceiling.

'D-d-dead,' whispered E.J.

3
SAM FOX, YOUR NUMBER IS UP

I freed the American cub scout and helped him out to join the six Australian ones.

'Nobody is to come *anywhere near* the bus,' I told them.

Then I went back for Mum.

'Have you had a look at Mr Johnson?' she asked. She must have heard me talking to E.J.

'I'm getting you out first,' I said in my Baloo voice – I wasn't going to argue about it. '*Then* I'll check on Mr Johnson.'

There was a creaking noise. The bus shuddered.

'What was that?' Mum gasped.

I told her what was going on as I positioned myself underneath her. Mum was much bigger than a nine-year-old cub, so I had to lie on my back and lower her down on top of me. Then I couldn't move – Mum was too heavy and we were sandwiched between the upside-down seat backs and the squashed-in ceiling. We stared at each other, our faces only a few centimetres apart. Our situation might have been funny if our lives weren't in danger. And if Mr Johnson wasn't only a few metres away, either dead or badly injured.

'Can you crawl over me?' I asked.

Mum nodded. But when she tried lifting herself up, her body went rigid and she let out a little grunt of pain.

'Mum! What's the matter?'

'Nothing,' she said through gritted teeth.

I knew she was lying. She had another injury – something worse than the cut on her head. It was hurting her to move. But she had to move – our lives depended on it.

A centimetre at a time, Mum wriggled across me. Finally she dragged herself out through the shattered window. As soon as she was clear, I rolled over and crawled out after her.

Behind us, the bus made a creaking noise and another small avalanche went clattering down the cliff.

'We've got to get Mr Johnson out,' Mum said.

She tried to stand up, but lost her balance. I had to grab her to stop her falling against the side of the bus and sending it crashing down into the river below.

'You'd better sit down, Mum,' I said. 'I'll see about Mr Johnson.'

It wasn't something I was looking forward to. The front of the bus was crumpled up like a squashed drink can. I didn't think anyone could be in there and still be alive.

Fearing the worst, I knelt down and put my eye to the narrow slot that used to be the driver's window. Another eye looked back at me.

And blinked.

'Are you all right?' I asked.

It was a stupid thing to say. Of course Mr Johnson wasn't all right. But I was still suffering from a mild case of shock myself. It had only been about ten minutes since the accident.

'Leg . . . stuck,' Mr Johnson groaned.

'Don't worry,' I said in my confident Baloo voice. 'I'll get you out.'

I scrambled around the front of the bus, searching for a way in. And stopped dead.

Hooley dooley! Half of the bus's front section hung in mid-air, dangling over a 50-metre drop. My toes were only centimetres from the edge.

I can handle a lot of things – fighting off wild animals, for example – but I can't handle heights. Every muscle in my body went into complete shutdown. I couldn't move.

But I *was* moving. The ground sloped down sharply towards the cliff's edge and gravity was pulling at the dirt beneath my trainers, making me slide forwards.

Snap out of it, said the little voice in my head, *or you'll wind up splattered like strawberry jam at the bottom of the cliff!*

It spurred me into action. I grabbed hold of the bus's bumper to stop my slide. But the bus was balanced on a knife edge. There was a loud grinding noise, metal against rock, and the bus started tipping. And when the bus tipped, so did I. There was nothing I could do.

My weight was pushing the bus over the edge, but if I let go, I'd fall.

The bus kept slowly tipping until I was leaning right out over the dizzying vertical drop. The toes of my trainers sent a trail of pebbles and small rocks spiralling down towards the wiggly blue line of the river far below. It was like looking down from an aeroplane.

An aeroplane that was about to crash.

Sam Fox, your number is up! screamed the little voice in my head.

Suddenly the bus stopped tipping.

Thumpthumpthumpthumpthumpthump went my racing heart.

Then, like a giant seesaw, the bus started tipping the other way, pulling me back to an upright position.

'We've got you, Baloo,' someone said behind me.

Four hands grabbed the back of my shirt and pulled.

I fell backwards onto the ground between Guy and Sally.

'Thanks, guys,' I gasped.

Sally hiccupped. 'It wasn't just us,' she said.

Spaced along the uphill side of the bus, each gripping

19

a wheel or part of the crumpled bodywork, were Joel, Emma and Matt. They'd pulled the teetering bus back from the brink. They'd saved my life.

'Thanks, Gunggari Pack,' I said, struggling upright. My legs felt wobbly and I was shaking all over, but there wasn't time to sit down and recover. 'Hold the bus steady while I free Mr Johnson.'

'Is he O-O-OK?' stammered E.J., still sitting on the grassy slope next to Mum and Will.

'His leg's stuck,' I said. 'I'm going in to get him.'

Mum had a bloodstained scarf tied around her head like a bandage. 'Do you need help?' she asked.

'No. There's only room for one person.'

It was true. The only way to get to Mr Johnson was through the shattered windscreen. Provided I could fit. The front window was squashed into a narrow, jelly-bean shape. And half of it projected over the cliff.

Don't look down, I told myself.

While the five uninjured members of the Gunggari Pack held the bus steady, I used a rock to bash away the remaining glass. Then I wormed headfirst into the crumpled driver's compartment.

Mr Johnson lay on his back. His right leg was jammed between the dashboard and a black metal lump that had smashed down through the floor above him. The lump was covered with oil and looked like part of the engine.

'Can you move, Mr Johnson?'

'I think . . . my leg's . . . broken,' he said weakly.

Mr Johnson was wearing shorts. His thigh looked like a section of black-and-blue sausage caught in a giant rat trap. I put my feet against the upside-down dashboard and pushed with all my strength. But it wouldn't budge.

'Lever . . .' gasped Mr Johnson, rolling his eyes sideways.

It took me a moment to understand. There was a thin iron bar poking out from behind Mr Johnson's seat. I carefully wriggled it free. The bar was nearly a metre long, with two right-angle bends, like a wonky Z, at one end. I poked the straight end into the gap between the dashboard and the engine and tried to pry them apart. But the gap didn't get any wider. Mr Johnson's leg was still firmly stuck.

Suddenly there were noises outside – muffled exclamations and scuffling sounds. The bus wobbled.

'Hey, Guy, what's going on?' I called.

He didn't answer.

'Guy?' I said, louder this time.

No answer. Just the scuffling sounds growing fainter. Like feet running away. The bus wobbled again.

'*GUY!*' I shouted.

I was wasting my breath. Guy and the others were no longer there. They'd run away. Left me and Mr Johnson teetering on the edge of the cliff.

Left us to die!

Then I heard Mum's voice. 'Sam,' she called softly, 'whatever you do, don't come out of the bus.'

'Why not?' I asked.

'There's a bear just outside.'

4
ATTACK

The bus shook. From behind us came snuffly breathing, like a baby with a cold. A very big baby.

'I think it's . . . inside . . . the bus,' whispered Mr Johnson.

My skin prickled. Twisting my head around, I peered through the wreckage into the rear section of the overturned vehicle.

Shishkebab!

The bear was only two metres away. Its head and shoulders completely filled one of the broken windows. It was trying to push its way in. But the crumpled window frame wasn't big enough. Every time the bear pushed, the bus tipped a few degrees further out over the 50-metre drop that yawned below us.

'It's . . . black,' wheezed Mr Johnson.

I gave him a blank look, wondering what difference the bear's colour made.

'. . . not grizzly.'

Now I understood. It wasn't a grizzly, it was a black bear. They aren't dangerous like grizzlies. They're scared of humans!

I drew in my breath. And yelled at the bear at the top of my voice. *'YAAAAAAAAAAAAAAAAH!'*

The bear looked right at me. It made a hoarse coughing sound, like the bark of a very old dog, then dragged its head out of the window frame.

'Holy guacamole!' I muttered, my heart pounding like a drum. 'I thought we were toast!'

'Hasn't . . . gone . . . away,' Mr Johnson whispered.

The bus started wobbling again. The bear was back. It was trying to get in through one of the windows further down the bus.

'YAAAAAAH!' I yelled, waving my hands. *'SHOO! SCRAM! BUZZ OFF!'*

This time the bear took no notice. Wet nostrils twitching, it stretched its long pale snout further and further inside the bus. I heard tree roots creaking. The bus rocked like a boat.

I yelled and screamed at the bear to go away, but it seemed obsessed with getting into the bus.

'Wants . . . cordial,' Mr Johnson croaked.

A bear's sense of smell is 20 times more powerful than a human's. And they love sweet things. It must have smelled the spilled cordial and come to investigate. But the pool of sugary red liquid was just out of reach. To get to it, the bear would have to push itself all the way into the bus. The extra weight would tip us over the edge.

I had to stop the bear before it killed us. But shouting was no good – the smell of the raspberry cordial was too enticing. I'd have to use force.

Poking the iron bar through the narrow gap beneath Mr Johnson's seat back, I tried to prod the bear. But even at full stretch, I couldn't quite reach it.

Time for Plan B.

'Wait here, Mr Johnson,' I said. Which was a pretty dumb thing to say, because what else could he do?

Pushing the iron bar ahead of me, I wriggled out through the broken windscreen onto the cliff top. I stood up and took a deep breath to steady my nerves. Then I walked around the side of the bus.

The bear didn't see me coming. Its head was inside the bus. I walked up beside it and tapped it with the iron bar.

Black bears, like most wild animals, avoid humans when they can. But if you corner them or give them a fright, they can turn nasty.

As quick as a startled snake, the bear reversed out of the bus and whirled around.

'Whuuuuuff!' it barked, showering me with spit.

I took off in the other direction.

Bears are noisy when they run. They huff and puff like steam trains. Their feet thump like horses' hooves. So I didn't need to look over my shoulder to know that the bear was right behind me. Closing in fast.

I was dimly aware of voices shouting advice at me: *Look out! Drop to the ground and cover your head! Climb a tree!*

But the loudest voice came from inside my head.

It was my karate instructor, Mr Habarty, talking to me before my first inter-club competition five years earlier. 'Remember, Sam – attack is the best means of defence.'

I wondered if Mr Habarty had ever been attacked by a 200-kilogram bear.

But this was a *black* bear, not a grizzly. They were supposed to be afraid of humans. I spun around and whacked it with the iron bar.

Or tried to. There wasn't time to take aim. Instead of connecting with the bear's head, the crooked end of the bar got tangled in its legs. The bear tripped and steamrolled right over the top of me.

OOOFF!

The animal was thickly padded with fur and autumn fat. Even though it was huge, I wasn't hurt. Just a bit winded and bruised. I staggered to my feet. The bear was three metres away, staggering to *its* feet. It made an angry blowing sound through its rubbery lips and rose up on its hind legs. It was taller than me.

Attack is the best means of defence. Thanks to Mr Habarty's advice, I made it to the semi-finals at my first inter-club karate competition. But the iron bar lay on the ground behind the bear. My only weapons were my bare hands.

I raised them in front of me.

'YAAAAAAH!' I yelled.

And walked straight towards the bear.

5
CLIMB, BALOO!

The bear watched me walk towards it. I took one . . .
two . . . three small, shaky steps.

It didn't move.

Please run away, bear! I begged it in my mind.

Four steps, five steps.

The closer I got, the bigger the bear looked.

Six . . . seven . . .

Finally, when we were almost close enough to shake
hands, the bear made a huffing sound, dropped onto
all fours, turned and went shambling away along the
cliff top.

Phew!

'That was the bravest – *hic!* – thing I've ever seen!' Sally said from three-quarters of the way up a fir tree.

Guy clung to the branch above her. 'Baloo rules!' he cried.

A chorus of cubs' voices echoed him from the nearby trees: 'Baloo rules! Baloo rules! Baloo rules!'

Only Mum and Will were still on the ground. They'd hidden behind a large rock, which was probably just as safe as the trees because black bears are excellent climbers.

'Did it hurt you?' Mum asked.

'I'm OK,' I said, even though my insides felt like jelly and my legs were so wobbly I could barely walk in a straight line.

There was the loud bang of a tree root breaking. We all looked at the bus. It shuddered, then tipped further towards the river below.

'*DAAAAAAAAD!*' yelled E.J.

'Everybody down from the trees!' I ordered, scooping up the iron bar and hurrying towards the bus as fast as my wobbly legs would take me. 'We have to get Mr Johnson out *now!*'

Even Mum and E.J. helped this time. Everyone held the bus steady while I crawled in with the iron bar to free Mr Johnson.

'Where's the jack?' I asked him.

While I was fighting the bear, I'd realised what the bar was for. It was the handle for cranking up the jack when the bus had a flat tyre.

'Under . . . my seat,' Mr Johnson said weakly.

The bus was upside down. So the jack was no longer *under* Mr Johnson's seat, it was *above* it. I reached up and carefully wriggled it free. It was almost identical to the one in my big brother's four-wheel drive. I positioned it next to Mr Johnson's trapped leg in the gap between the dashboard and the engine. Then I fitted the square end of the bar into the socket that operated the jack, and started turning the handle.

CRE-E-E-E-A-AK!

Mr Johnson let out a groan.

I stopped cranking. 'Are you all right?'

'Yes,' he gasped. 'It's . . . coming . . . loose! Keep . . . winding!'

I got back to work, cranking the jack handle as fast as

I could. Slowly the gap came open, like a wide, smiling mouth.

CRE-E-E-E-E-A-AK!

Then there was another sound – a loud, splintering snap – followed by a series of thumps, bumps and crashes that ended with a distant splash.

A tremor ran through the bus.

'Sam, hurry!' Mum shouted from outside. 'One of the trees just fell over the cliff. There's almost nothing holding the bus now!'

I gave the handle a final 360-degree turn, then tossed it to one side. Mr Johnson's leg was free. But it looked a mess. It was black and blue. There was a big lump just above the knee, a sure sign that it was broken. It needed a splint, but there wasn't time for first aid. I gripped Mr Johnson around the waist.

'I'm going to pull you out,' I said.

He nodded and gritted his teeth.

But before I could start pulling, the bus gave a big lurch and started to tip. Mr Johnson rolled sideways, pinning me against the crumpled ceiling. There were shouts from outside. They couldn't hold the bus. It was going over the edge!

A stream of red liquid trickled past my ear. For a second I thought it was blood, then I smelt raspberry cordial. The cubs and Mum were yelling advice, but I couldn't hear what they were saying. I was too busy wriggling out from under Mr Johnson. His body had gone limp. I wrapped my arms around his chest and wriggled towards the narrow strip of light shining in through the bus's flattened windscreen. Broken glass crunched under my shoulder. I bumped my head on something. The bus felt like a capsizing ship. I didn't know which way was up and which was down.

Outside, tree roots snapped like gunshots. Someone screamed my name. Focusing on the strip of light, I hauled Mr Johnson after me. He was so heavy! Hands appeared in the gap. Lots of hands. With a final, desperate heave, I shoved Mr Johnson towards the hands. They grabbed him. His big, floppy body squeezed through the gap and disappeared.

I tried to follow, but something was holding me back. My jeans were snagged. I couldn't get out! I was trapped in the bus and it was tipping, tipping, tipping . . . Going over the edge. Taking me with it!

There was a loud bang, then a tearing sound, and the bus broke free. Time seemed to stand still. I felt weightless, like at the top of a roller-coaster ride.

There wasn't time to think. Just to act. Aiming my head and shoulders at the windscreen gap, I kicked with my legs, propelling my body towards the light.

RIIIIIIIIIIIIP! went my jeans.

I was out of the bus. I was flying. A branch flashed past. I grabbed hold with both hands. It nearly tore my arms out of their sockets, but I held on. Held on for my life.

Don't look down, I told myself. But I looked down anyway.

A toy bus was below me. It was in free fall. I watched it getting smaller and smaller and smaller, until it hit the toy river and exploded.

There was nothing 'toy' about the explosion.

BOOOOOOOM!

The shock wave was like a blast of hot air from a furnace. It took my breath away.

'Sam!'

I looked up. Mum and a line of cub scouts stood silhouetted against the sky at the top of the cliff. I was ten metres below them, dangling from an upside-down tree. It was one of the two fir trees that had been supporting the bus. The other one had fallen down the cliff. All that was keeping mine from following it was a single, splintered root not much thicker than my wrist. I could see it through a gap in the branches. And I could see the root fibres snapping one by one, like the strands of a badly frayed rope that was about to break.

'CLIMB, BALOO!' yelled the cubs.

6
GRAND HOWL

The tree bounced off the cliff face four times on the way down, then smashed into wood chips on the rocks beside the flaming wreck of the bus.

'Lucky you weren't still holding on to it, Baloo,' said Sally. Her hiccups had stopped.

My hands shook as I dusted twigs and bits of bark off my scout leader's uniform. There was raspberry cordial all over my shirt, and the back pocket of my jeans had been ripped off. 'Yeah, lucky,' I said.

But I had a bad feeling that we weren't out of danger yet.

Mum must have had the same feeling. 'Pack meeting!'

she called from the grassy slope, where Joel was helping E.J. make two tree-branch splints for Mr Johnson's broken leg. We gathered around her in a semicircle.

'First, I want to congratulate everyone for the way you've behaved today,' Mum said. 'You've all been very brave and looked out for each other the way cubs are supposed to.'

'Wasn't it cool how Baloo chased away the bear?' Sally interrupted. 'He should get a bravery award.'

Mum smiled in my direction. With the scarf around her head and streaks of dried blood on her face, she looked like a pirate. 'I'm very proud of Baloo,' she said. 'I'm proud of everyone. You all deserve bravery awards.'

'Emma should get a first-aid award, too,' said Will, whose injured arm was supported in a sling made from a pink sweatshirt.

'Definitely,' said Mum. 'But let's not worry about awards right now. Does anyone have a mobile phone?'

There were head shakes all round.

'What about food?' Mum asked. 'Has anyone got any trail mix, lollies, chocolate bars?'

More head shakes.

'Or drinks?' Mum's eyes travelled hopefully around the group of silent cubs. 'I don't suppose anyone brought their water bottles when they got out of the bus?'

Same result. Just a semicircle of shaking heads. Nobody had drink, nobody had food, nobody had a mobile phone. All our gear had gone over the cliff with the bus.

'Are we lost, Akela?' asked Matt beside me.

'No, Matt, we aren't lost,' Mum said. She pointed up the hill. 'The road's just up there. But Mr Johnson can't walk and it's much too steep to carry him.'

'I'll go up and stop a car,' I volunteered. 'I'll get them to call an ambulance.'

Mum nodded. 'That's a good idea, Baloo. Take someone with you.'

'Who wants to come?' I asked.

Several hands shot up. I chose Guy.

'Awwww!' said Sally, who'd had both hands up.

'I'll pick you next time,' I promised.

'When a car stops,' Mum said to me, 'see if they've got any water to spare.'

I gave her the scout salute, then Guy and I set off up the side of the canyon. We followed the avenue of broken saplings and flattened undergrowth carved through the forest by the bus when it had come crashing down from the road. It was only 50 or 60 metres, but the slope was so steep that it took us nearly five minutes to make the short climb.

The condition of the road surprised me. I hadn't taken much notice when we'd been driving along it in the bus – I'd been too busy looking for grizzly bears. But now, standing on its dusty, pot-holed surface, I discovered it was little more than a logging trail. And a disused logging trail, at that. Apart from the zigzag tread pattern of the bus's tyres, which veered suddenly and disappeared over the edge, and the huge hoof prints of the moose that had caused the accident, there were no other marks in the dust.

'No one's driven along here for ages,' I said.

'Except Mr Johnson,' said Guy.

And look what happened to Mr Johnson, I thought.

We waited for nearly an hour, but both of us knew it was a waste of time. No cars were going to come. It was an unused road.

'What'll we do?' Guy asked finally.

I shrugged. 'I guess we'd better go back and give Akela and the others the bad news.'

At least we wouldn't have to go back empty-handed. Thirty metres from where we'd been waiting, a slow trickle of water seeped out of a clay embankment and formed a small pool at the road's edge. The water looked clear. I sniffed it, then tasted it – it seemed OK. Guy found a dusty hub cap that had fallen off the bus when it went over the edge. We gave it a rinse, then filled it with water to take back for the others.

Mum was pleased we'd found water, but disappointed when we told her about the road.

'My fault,' said Mr Johnson, taking slow sips from the hub cap as I held it to his lips. 'I was taking . . . a short cut. No traffic . . . comes this way. You'll have to . . . walk back . . . to the main highway.'

Mr Johnson wasn't sure how far we'd come from the highway. Ten kilometres, he reckoned. If I jogged, I could do it in an hour.

Mum called another pack meeting. 'Baloo is going back to the highway to get help,' she said. 'I want one volunteer to go with him.'

'No, Mum,' I said. 'I'll go on my own.'

'It isn't safe, Sam. I'd be happier if someone went with you.'

'But the cubs will slow me down.'

'It doesn't matter.' Mum switched to her scout leader voice. 'I want you to take someone with you, Baloo.'

'I'm a good runner,' said Sally. 'I came third in our whole school in the cross-country.'

I shook my head. 'I'm sorry, Sally, but I choose Guy.'

'But you promised!'

'You did promise, Baloo,' Mum reminded me.

'OK, then,' I said, and gave Guy an apologetic look.

E.J. stepped forward. 'I want to go, too.'

'No, E.J. You should stay here and help look after your dad,' I said.

'I want to go with you,' he said stubbornly. 'This is America. I live here, you don't.'

Mum caught my eye. 'He's right, Baloo. You might find E.J's local knowledge helpful.'

'And I've got this,' E.J. said, pulling a small Swiss Army knife from one of his pockets. 'It's got blades for almost everything.'

'That's settled, then,' Mum said. She gathered everyone around her. 'Gunggari Pack, let's send E.J, Sally and Baloo off with the Grand Howl.'

We all filled our lungs and howled.

From somewhere deep in the mountains around us, another – much eerier – howl came echoing back. It was the spookiest sound I'd ever heard.

'What was *that*?' said Guy, his eyes bulging in fright.

E.J. looked scared, too.

'Real wolves,' he whispered.

7
BIGFOOT!

'Are wolves dangerous?' Sally asked ten minutes later.

The three of us were walking down the bumpy dirt road in the direction of the highway. We all carried big sticks and kept glancing into the forest on either side of us.

'You betcha they're dangerous,' E.J. said. 'A pack of wolves can bring down a fully grown moose.'

'Do they attack people?' asked Sally.

'Only if they're really hungry,' E.J. said. 'And if the person isn't in a group with other people.'

Now I was glad that Mum had insisted I take E.J. and Sally with me. 'So three people's a safe number?' I said.

Before E.J. could answer, Sally let out a little gasp and grabbed my arm.

'What's the matter?' I asked.

Instead of answering, she pointed into the forest on the uphill side of the road. I caught a glimpse of greyish-brown fur between two trees, but when I focused on the spot, nothing was there but branches and leaves. One of the branches was swaying slightly.

Sally's fingers dug into my arm. 'Did you see it?' she whispered.

'I saw something furry,' I said. 'Was it a wolf?'

She shook her head. 'It was a person, I think. Except it was covered in fur.'

Now it was E.J. who gasped.

'Bigfoot!' he said.

8
SNAP!

People who've seen Bigfoot describe it as a huge ape-like creature, nearly twice the size of a gorilla, that walks upright like a human. There have been lots of sightings, going right back to the days when Europeans first settled in North America. And even before that, Native Americans called it the Sasquatch. But modern-day scientists don't think Bigfoot is real. They reckon the sightings are hoaxes, or people mistaking bears for giant apes.

That's what I believed, too. Until now. In my head was a picture of Bigfoot – half-man, half-ape, three metres tall.

It was something I absolutely did not want to meet.

'Should we go back and warn the others?' whispered Sally.

Part of me wanted to. We could be back there in ten minutes. But every second was precious. We had to reach the highway and get help for Mum and Mr Johnson and Will before nightfall.

'I don't think Bigfoot's dangerous,' I said.

E.J. looked up into the forest where Sally and I had glimpsed Bigfoot. 'A little boy disappeared from a camp site a few years back. It wasn't far from here. People reckon Bigfoot got him.'

Trust E.J. to make things worse.

'You two can go back if you like,' I said, gripping my stick so hard my knuckles turned white. 'I'm going to the highway.'

'I'll go with you, Baloo,' said Sally.

'Me, too,' said E.J.

We walked faster after that. And kept glancing over our shoulders, half-expecting to see Bigfoot following us.

But the danger wasn't behind us.

'Yikes!' said Sally.

We'd just come around a corner. About 100 metres away, a bear was crossing the road. It looked enormous – much bigger than the black bear we'd seen earlier – and its fur was brown.

We stopped in our tracks.

The bear stopped, too, and turned its broad, shaggy head in our direction.

'It's a grizzly,' E.J. whispered.

'Should we lie on the ground?' asked Sally.

'That's only if they attack,' whispered E.J. 'Walk backwards – slowly, so it doesn't think we're running away.'

Step by step, we backed away from the grizzly. It was hard not to run. I'd heard lots of stories about grizzlies and none of them were good. They're the most dangerous and unpredictable of all bears. They kill more humans than any other wild animal in North America. They're ten times stronger than a man.

Our sticks would be totally useless if it attacked.

Please don't attack, I thought, as Sally, E.J. and I shuffled backwards along the disused logging road. We'd nearly reached the corner.

Suddenly, I felt a light breeze on the back of my neck. Uh oh! It would carry our scent to the grizzly. I wondered if grizzlies could smell fear.

I saw it raise its muzzle in the air.

Then it turned slowly and came walking up the road towards us.

'Now do we lie down?' asked Sally.

She was braver than me. No way was I going to lie down.

'I think we should run,' I whispered.

E.J. shook his head. 'That'll make *it* run.'

He was right. The grizzly was still 60 metres away, but I'd seen how fast bears could move when they wanted to. It was *walking* almost as fast as I could run. With every step it took, the gap between the grizzly and us was closing by about a metre. It would catch us in under a minute.

'What'll we do?' I asked.

'Climb a tree,' whispered E.J.

'Can't grizzlies climb trees?' asked Sally.

'Not like black bears,' E.J. whispered. 'They're too big and heavy.'

We backed slowly around the corner. As soon as we were out of sight, E.J. turned and said, '*Run*!'

The trees in the Rocky Mountains are ideal for climbing. They have tall, straight trunks with lots of branches that poke out like the rungs of a ladder. Which was lucky for us. Because no sooner had we reached the nearest trees and started climbing, than the grizzly came charging around the corner. It didn't even pause to look for us. Its nose told it where we were. Without breaking its stride, the huge shaggy bear swerved off the road and came lumbering towards us.

There hadn't been much time to choose our trees. Sally and E.J. were lucky. Their trees were tall. Mine was only six metres high, with a trunk hardly thicker than a man's thigh. The grizzly must have weighed half a tonne. It hit my skinny tree at full speed.

WHOMP!

Luckily, I was holding on tight. The tree bent like a whip, then sprang back the other way, knocking the grizzly over backwards. It landed in a big furry heap, and didn't move for a couple of seconds. Then it raised its head and looked around. It seemed slightly dazed.

Flies buzzed around its nose and eyes, and a long line of drool dangled from its mouth. Slowly, the huge bear struggled to its feet. It came ambling back to the base of my tree and looked up. Our eyes met. Go away, bear, I thought. But the grizzly had other ideas.

Making an angry puffing sound, like someone blowing on hot soup, it started climbing up after me.

E.J. reckoned grizzlies *couldn't* climb trees! I scrambled away from it, clambering up through the branches until I was nearly at the top. The trunk got really skinny. It started swaying back and forth, making an ominous creaking sound. But the grizzly kept coming. Higher and higher, closer and closer.

Sally's and E.J.'s trees were on either side of mine. They started throwing fir cones at the grizzly, but that just made it more determined. Puffing and snorting, the huge, shaggy bear fought its way upwards until its head was just below my feet. I thought about kicking it in the nose, but one look at its enormous yellow teeth made me change my mind.

I had no choice but to climb a little higher.

CREEEEEEAK!

Slowly, the tree started bending. The grizzly and I went with it. There was nothing I could do but hold on. This time the tree didn't reach a point where it swayed back the other way. It kept bending, further and further, until . . .

SNAP!

9
BEAR HUG

E.J. was right – grizzlies *are* too big to climb trees. A branch snapped beneath the bear's enormous weight, sending it crashing to the ground. It landed with a thump, rolled down the steep hillside and crashed into a boulder.

Grizzlies are tough. It wasn't hurt. It sat up, shook the dust off itself, then came ambling back to the tree, which had sprung upright again as soon as the bear fell.

'Buzz off,' I said.

The grizzly's nose twitched, sniffing the air. It must have liked what it smelled, because it rose up on its hind legs and regarded me with its small, piggy eyes.

And licked its chops.

It's a really creepy feeling being looked at like you're food. It sent a shiver down my spine.

'YAAAAAAAAH!' I yelled, trying the same tactic I'd used on the other bear.

But this was a grizzly, not a black bear. Yelling just made it mad. It wrinkled its nose and lifted its upper lip, giving me another look at its fearsome teeth. I was worried it would try climbing up after me again, but the grizzly had a different plan. Gripping the tree in a bear hug, it started pushing and pulling at the trunk. It was trying to shake me down. The tree wobbled and shook. The top part of it – where I was – swayed sickeningly from side to side. I held on tight and prayed that the skinny trunk wouldn't break.

Suddenly, there was a popping sound. The tree gave a big jolt. I looked down.

Shishkebab! The tree's roots were pulling out of the ground. One by one, they broke free of the dusty soil. The tree started leaning. Sensing what was happening, the grizzly shook it even harder. More roots broke free, popping out of the ground like long, knobbly fingers.

Almost in slow motion, the tree began to fall. I felt myself tipping backwards. My luck had run out. If the fall didn't kill me, the grizzly certainly would.

'Grab a branch!' a voice said.

I'd stopped tipping. E.J. was directly above me. His face was red and sweaty as he gripped the very top of my tree with one hand. His other arm was wrapped securely around the trunk of his own tree. My tree must have toppled into his and he'd grabbed it, halting its fall.

'Hurry!' he gasped. 'I can't hold on much longer!'

I swung myself from my tree into E.J's tree just as E.J. lost his grip. The smaller tree crashed to the ground, leaving me dangling from a branch two metres below E.J.

It was a long thin branch and I was right at the end of it. I heard a familiar creaking sound and the branch started to bend downwards. I went with it. There were no other branches within reach. All I could do was hold on, grit my teeth and wait for the branch to snap.

CREEEEEEEAK!

It didn't snap. It bent like a fishing rod, all the way

down until my feet touched the ground.

Uh oh!

I desperately tried to haul myself back up. But I was too slow. A huge paw came out of nowhere – *pow!* – and sent me flying.

10
DANGEROUS
PLACE

Two pieces of advice flashed through my brain as the grizzly loomed over me – *lie face down on the ground and cover your head* and *attack is the best means of defence.*

But before I could decide, a large grey-and-white dog leapt across me and buried its teeth in the grizzly's shoulder. A second dog came from the side, hitting the bear in the ribs. With a roar of anger, the grizzly rose up on its hind legs and swatted its attackers away, only to be hit from behind by two more.

Suddenly there were big pale dogs everywhere, hurling themselves at the bear from all directions. I thought they were huskies until one landed on top of me. For a few trembling heartbeats, the animal straddled my chest. There was no mistaking that long, tapering muzzle and those golden-yellow eyes.

I was nose-to-nose with a wolf.

One snap of those fearsome jaws could have severed my jugular vein. But it wasn't me the wolves were after, it was the grizzly. With a low, dog-like growl, the wolf whirled around and launched itself back into the fray.

I curled up in a ball, making myself as small as possible, as the battle raged. It was like being in a rugby scrum, but instead of boots and elbows and knees, there were claws and paws and flashing teeth. I was showered in flying spit. Clumps of fur fell all around me. Most of it was grey and white. The wolves had the numbers, but the grizzly had the power. I heard a yelp of pain, and a wolf hit the ground in a cloud of dust. Another wolf had blood on its leg.

Someone was shouting at me. I recognised Sally's voice.

'BALOO! CLIMB A TREE!'

It was good advice. Neither the bear nor the wolves were taking any notice of me; they were too busy fighting each other. I crawled away from the battle towards the nearest tree trunk. Sally was right above me, motioning at me to climb up.

I don't think I've ever climbed a tree so fast.

'They're going,' Sally said as soon as I reached her.

I looked down. The wolves were filing into the forest in a long, ragged line. There were about 12 of them. Two at the rear of the pack were limping, another had a badly torn ear. The grizzly had won the battle. It lumbered after them for a few seconds, making a loud *huff-huff-huff* sound like a steam train, then it stopped and sat down.

'Were they wolves?' Sally asked.

I nodded. I was watching them vanish silently into the trees. 'Why did they attack the bear?' I wondered out loud.

'Who cares?' Sally said. 'They saved your life.'

She was right. Thanks to the wolves, I was still alive. The grizzly would have killed me for sure if they hadn't come along. But the danger wasn't over yet. The grizzly was still there, sitting on the ground not far from our tree, licking one of its front paws.

'I think it's hurt,' I whispered.

'Good,' said Sally.

Partly I agreed with her. The grizzly had tried to kill me. And it had beaten up several of the wolves. But they had attacked it, so it had a good excuse. I still didn't understand what the fight had been about. Was it something to do with food? Did the wolves attack the bear so they could get me? If that was the case, then I owed my life to the grizzly!

'Hey, Baloo, are you OK?' E.J. called from his tree.

'I'm fine,' I said softly, still watching the bear. I wanted to ask E.J. if wolves often attacked grizzlies, but I didn't want to attract the bear's attention. It had turned its head when E.J. called out to me.

Now it stood up and came ambling back in our direction. It stopped right under Sally and me, and looked up. Its black muzzle quivered. Goose bumps prickled my skin.

'I think I'm the one it's after,' I whispered.

The grizzly rose up on its hind legs and began climbing the tree.

'Yikes!' said Sally.

I was about to tell her to climb a bit higher, when a long, wailing howl rose out of the forest nearby. Wolves.

The grizzly stopped climbing and looked in the direction of the eerie sound. For four or five seconds the bear didn't move a muscle, then it snorted, dropped nimbly to the ground and went ambling off down the road.

As soon as the grizzly had gone, the wolves stopped howling.

'Thank you, wolves,' Sally whispered.

We stayed in the trees for another 15 minutes, until we were sure neither the bear nor the wolves were coming back. Then Sally and I climbed cautiously back down and stood at the edge of the road.

'Now what, Baloo?' E.J. asked, walking across from his tree to join us.

'Call me Sam,' I said. I wished I wasn't the one who had to make the decisions. 'Do you think it's safe to keep going?'

'Akela sent us to get help.'

But things had changed. I looked down at the road's

dusty surface. The bear's paw prints were the size of dinner plates. 'The grizzly's somewhere ahead of us.'

'And Bigfoot's behind us,' said Sally.

I'd forgotten about that. Bigfoot, grizzlies, wolves – America was a dangerous place.

'There might be another way,' E.J. said. 'We can get help at the farm.'

'What farm?' I asked, surprised. We were surrounded by forest and mountains.

E.J. waved one hand vaguely at the wall of spiky fir trees that bordered the road. 'It's about five kilometres that-a-way. You can see it from the tree I climbed.'

I scrambled up to have a look. Sure enough, there was a green patch of grassland at the far end of the valley. I could even see the red roof of a farmhouse. Awesome! Our troubles were nearly over.

But when I looked out over the undulating sea of forest between me and the farm, I had a sudden reality check. First we had to get there. E.J. reckoned it was five kilometres. That mightn't sound far, but finding our way through five kilometres of untamed wilderness wasn't going to be easy.

I climbed back down to join the others. 'What time does it get dark, E.J.?'

'Around eight.'

It was four o'clock now. 'We'd better get moving,' I said.

11
SHHHHH! IT'LL HEAR US!

For the first hour and a half we made quite good time. The forest floor was steep in places, but we were travelling downhill and there were no cliffs like further up the valley where the bus had crashed. The trees hid the farm from view, but I used the sun as my compass. As long as we kept it on our left, we were going in roughly the right direction. But as the afternoon wore on, we began to lose sight of the sun. Finally it disappeared behind the mountains, throwing the valley into shadow.

The forest was changing, too. The fir trees of the higher slopes gradually gave way to smaller trees with spreading branches and yellow autumn leaves. In places there were stands of saplings that grew so close together we had to go around them. It became impossible to walk in a straight line. We were continually taking detours around thickets, fallen logs and prickly brambles. E.J. pointed out a patch of tall, hairy-stemmed plants called burn weed.

'Keep away from those,' he warned. 'You'll be itching for hours.'

Without the sun as a guide, all we could do was keep heading downhill and hope we would reach the river soon. My plan then was to follow the river. It would lead us down the valley to the farm.

But first we had to *find* the river.

'You guys take a break,' I said, stopping beneath a tall, white-barked tree that looked like a poplar. 'I'm going to climb up and have a look around.'

'Are we lost?' asked E.J.

'No. I just want to see how far it is to the river.'

The poplar had looked easy to climb from the ground, but halfway up I got stuck. There were too many branches. I couldn't get through.

'Give me a go, Baloo,' Sally said from below. 'I'm smaller than you.'

I slithered back down and let her have a try. Sally was tall for a nine-year-old, but she was really skinny. She wriggled up through the branches like a human snake. All the way to the top.

'Can you see the farm?' asked E.J.

'No,' Sally said. 'I can only see trees.'

'What about the river?' I asked.

'I can't see the river, either.'

'You're looking in the wrong direction,' E.J. said.

He was right. Sally was staring back the way we'd come. Suddenly she let out a little gasp.

'Yikes! A grizzly!'

My skin prickled. E.J. and I looked in the direction Sally was looking, but of course we saw nothing. Only a thick wall of forest.

'Where is it?' I asked.

'Halfway up the hill,' Sally said. A tumble of yellow leaves fluttered to the ground as she clambered down through the branches. 'I only saw it for a second, but it looked like the same one. It was coming this way.'

I turned to E.J. 'Do you think it's after us?'

He shrugged. 'Let's not wait to find out.'

It was hard to move quickly through the forest. Thorny brambles scratched our legs and caught in our clothing. Leaves slapped in our faces. We scrambled over fallen logs and waded waist-deep through sweetfern.

Shhhhh! I kept thinking, every time one of us trod on a stick or rattled two branches together. *It'll hear us!*

But I didn't say it out loud. Because it was impossible to hurry *and* be quiet. Which got me thinking . . .

'Hey, guys,' I whispered. 'Stop for a moment. I want to hear if the grizzly's following us.'

We all stopped and listened. Sweat dribbled down our faces as we looked back the way we'd come. The forest was deathly silent.

'Can you guys hear anything?' E.J. whispered.

Sally and I shook our heads.

I turned to Sally. 'How far away was it?'

She shrugged. 'I don't know. I only saw it for a second.'

'Are you sure it was coming this way?' asked E.J.

Before Sally could answer, a stick snapped in the

forest nearby. It was followed, two seconds later, by the rustle of leaves.

That answered E.J.'s question.

'Run!' I hissed.

I could have saved my breath. E.J. and Sally were already running, crashing away through the trees and underbrush like two startled deer. I let them go ahead. I was Baloo. Their safety was my responsibility.

Attack is the best means of defence.

Scooping up a hefty stick, I turned and waited for the grizzly.

12
SNAPPER

There was a shout from deep in the woods behind me, followed by a high-pitched scream:

'BALOOOOOOOOOOOOOOO!'

Sally and E.J. were in trouble. I didn't hesitate. I whirled around and went charging off after them.

Here's what I thought as I ran ducking and weaving through the dense forest towards the sound of Sally's screams – the grizzly must have sneaked past me. Rather than face me and fight, it had made a detour through the woods and gone after my two smaller, weaker companions.

Coward! I thought. All the fear I'd been feeling

moments earlier was replaced by anger. I gripped the stick in both hands and charged towards an opening in the trees ahead. It looked like a clearing. That's where the screams were coming from.

It wasn't what I expected. There was no sign of the grizzly. Just Sally standing knee-deep near the edge of a small, weed-choked creek. She was leaning backwards, trying to pull something out of the muddy water.

'Baloo, help!' she screamed when she saw me.

'Coming!' I yelled, rattling through the rushes towards her. 'Where's E.J.?'

'He's *here*!' she cried.

Only when I reached the creek did I see E.J. Or part of him, anyway. Just his head and one arm were visible. The rest of him was underwater. His eyes were wide, his face was contorted, he was shivering. Sally had both hands wrapped around his wrist. She was trying to drag him towards the bank. But E.J. was sliding the other way.

Dropping my stick, I leapt into the creek and grabbed E.J.'s other hand.

'What's going on?' I puffed, still out of breath from my flat-out run through the forest.

'I was crossing the creek and a snapper got my foot,' he gasped.

I didn't know what a snapper was. Some kind of fish? It was really strong. Sally and I pulled E.J. one way, the snapper pulled the other. It was a tug of war. The snapper was winning. Our sneakers slipped down the muddy slope of the creek bed. The water got deeper and deeper. In another minute, E.J. would be completely underwater.

'Hold him while I get my shoes off,' I said to Sally.

She held on while I splashed back to the creek bank and ripped off my sneakers. It only took 15 seconds, but that was long enough for the snapper to gain another half-metre. E.J.'s face was barely above water when I ploughed back in and grabbed his arm again. There were tears in his eyes but he wasn't panicking. He had a lot of guts.

'Hang in there, E.J.,' I encouraged.

In bare feet I had more grip. The tables were turned. Centimetre by centimetre, Sally and I hauled E.J. into the shallows. As we neared the creek bank, I had my first view of the snapper. It was possibly the ugliest creature I'd ever seen (and I've seen a few!). It looked like a snake, with slimy green skin, a long pointy nose and gaping, pig-like nostrils. Its fearsome, beaked mouth was clamped firmly around E.J.'s right shoe.

Some kind of python? I wondered.

My question was soon answered as the rest of the snapper became visible. A large domed shell covered in pond slime rose out of the water. It wasn't a python, it was a huge old turtle.

The snapper was as big as a backpack and must have weighed 50 kilograms. Its horny feet were dug deep into the mud, resisting us every millimetre of the way. No matter how hard we tried, Sally and I couldn't get it up the steep, slippery bank onto dry land. I grabbed my stick and gave the turtle a whack. Instead of releasing E.J.'s foot as I'd hoped, the stubborn creature retracted its head into its shell, pulling the shoe in after it. I started bashing the shell.

'It won't let go,' E.J. grunted. 'Sometimes they hold on for 24 hours.'

'Where's your knife?' I gasped.

'In the water somewhere. I got it halfway out of my pocket but it slipped.'

'What if we try to get your foot out of the shoe?' Sally suggested.

It was E.J.'s only hope. I sat behind him with both arms around his chest and my heels buried in the mud, while Sally knelt in the shallow water to undo the laces. The shoe was pulled almost all the way into the turtle's shell, making it difficult to get at. But Sally had small hands and nimble fingers. She got the laces undone. E.J. twisted his ankle back and forth, and all three of us tugged, but the snapper held on.

'My foot feels swollen,' E.J. said. He gave a funny little laugh. 'I'm turning into Bigfoot!'

I was amazed he could joke about it. But this wasn't a time for jokes.

'Sally,' I said, 'take my place for a couple of minutes while I go and get something.'

Leaving her and E.J. at the edge of the creek, I grabbed one of my socks and dashed back towards the forest. And skidded to a halt.

Shishkebab!

The boy was crouched behind a tree. He looked about six years old. Straggly brown hair hung down to his waist and he was dressed from head to foot in animal furs.

'Where did you come from?' I asked.

'*Mwaa mwaa!*' said the boy. It sounded more like animal noise than talking. He waved one hand at me, then turned and went scampering into the forest on all fours like a monkey. Weird.

But there wasn't time to worry about him, or anything else that might be lurking in the woods – the grizzly, for example. I had to save E.J. Ever since he'd pointed out the burn weeds, I'd seen them growing everywhere. I found a plant now. Using my sock as a protective glove, I broke off a big handful of its hairy green leaves. But the sock wasn't very good protection. Halfway back to the creek, my hand started to sting. It felt like I was clutching a handful of red-hot pins. Yeowww! Now I knew where the plant got its name.

I dropped the burn weed and folded the sock back on itself to make a double layer. Then I stooped to pick up the leaves again.

Holy guacamole!

There were prints all over the ground. My footprints, the boy's footprints, and about a hundred big dog-like paw prints that could only have been made by wolves.

The grizzly wasn't the only animal following us.

My heart was still racing when I got back to Sally and E.J., but I tried to put what I'd just seen out of my mind. 'Do you think this'll work on the snapper, E.J.?' I asked, showing him the burn weed.

E.J. shook his head. 'Its skin's probably too thick.'

'What about the skin *inside* its mouth?'

I crushed the burn weed into a spongy green wad, then used the pointy end of my stick to push it into the tiny gap between the turtle's jaws and E.J.'s shoe.

Nothing happened. I washed my burning hand in the water and tried to think of another way to make the snapper let go. My fingers bumped something buried in the mud. E.J.'s pocket knife. I prised the longest blade open.

Sorry turtle, I thought.

But before I could use the knife, Sally let out a gasp.

'Yuck!' she said.

The snapper had started blowing green bubbles through its nose.

Then it opened its mouth and sneezed.

E.J. was free!

13
BEAR FOOD

'Man, oh man!' muttered E.J., gingerly removing his shoe as the snapper swam away. There was a big red line across the arch of his foot, surrounded by angry purple bruising. 'I think it's broken.'

'Are you serious?' I said.

'I'll see if I can stand up.'

Sally and I helped him to his feet. E.J. balanced on his good foot, then slowly transferred his weight to the other.

'Shoot!' he gasped. If Sally and I hadn't been supporting him, he would have collapsed in a heap.

We sat him back down.

'What are we going to do, Baloo?' Sally asked.

I began putting my shoes back on. 'I'll piggyback him.'

E.J. was nine years old and small for his age. He wasn't very heavy. We followed the bank of the muddy creek downstream. We kept looking over our shoulders. Nothing was following us. At least, nothing that we could see. In places, the forest came right down to the edge of the creek. Anything could be prowling through the trees.

I told E.J. and Sally about the paw prints and Cave Boy – that's what I called him, because of the animal skins.

'Maybe he's Bigfoot's kid,' E.J. suggested.

'He was human,' I said. 'Bigfoot's an animal.'

'Nobody knows for sure *what* Bigfoot is,' E.J. said.

I'd grown to like E.J. over the past couple of hours, but he could still get under my skin.

'He was just a normal-looking human boy, E.J.'

'Wearing animal skins.'

'Like Mowgli in *The Jungle Book*,' said Sally.

I stopped walking and lowered E.J. onto a log. I had just remembered something he'd said earlier.

'You know that little boy who disappeared from a camp site somewhere around here? It could be him.'

E.J. let out a low whistle. 'Fifty thousand dollars!'

'What are you talking about, E.J.?' asked Sally.

'There's a TV show called *Mystery Solvers*. If you help them solve a mystery – like finding that little orphan boy – they pay you fifty thousand dollars.'

'Was he an orphan?' I said.

'Yeah. It was really sad. His parents died in a car crash when he was two. He was being looked after by his uncle at the time he went missing,' explained E.J. He looked at Sally, then at me. 'We'll split the reward three ways.'

'But if Bigfoot kidnapped him,' Sally said, 'won't Bigfoot get really mad at anyone who tries to take the boy away?'

Whap!

Something hit me in the middle of my back.

'Ouch!' I cried, and spun around.

A big brown acorn lay in the dirt at my feet.

Clunk!

'Owwww!' yelped E.J., rubbing his knee.

A third flying acorn bounced off the log behind Sally.

'What's going on?' she cried.

'Someone's throwing acorns,' I said, ducking as another one sailed over our heads. They were coming from the trees over to our right. 'Let's get out of here.'

I loaded E.J. onto my back and set off along the bank of the creek at a fast jog. Sally could have run ahead, but she matched her pace with mine. Another acorn crashed into the rushes to our right and bounced harmlessly into the creek. We were nearly out of range.

'Wait till I get my hands on that kid!' muttered E.J.

'Did you see him?' I puffed.

'No.'

'Then how do you know it was him?' asked Sally.

'Who else would it be?'

'Bigfoot,' she said. 'Maybe it's trying to chase us away like a mother animal protecting its baby.'

E.J. twisted around to look behind us.

'Oh no!' he muttered.

Sally and I turned too, half-expecting to see Bigfoot. But it wasn't Bigfoot. It was the grizzly. I watched it amble out of the rushes about 200 metres away. It was following the exact path we'd taken, sniffing the rushes where we'd brushed past them. It was tracking us, all right.

The huge shaggy bear stopped near the log where we'd rested. It sniffed the log, then the ground, then it stood up on its hind legs and peered in our direction. We squatted down in the rushes so it couldn't see us.

'How fast can you run?' E.J. whispered in my ear.

I'm quite a good runner, but try running when you're bent over in a semi-crouch with someone on your back. After a couple of hundred metres, I was pooped. My leg muscles burned and I was right out of breath.

Luckily, the grizzly hadn't seen us. The rushes provided cover. But there was no hiding from that super-sensitive nose. We could hear it crunching through the rushes towards us, following our scent.

'We have to throw it off our trail,' I whispered, veering towards the creek.

'Watch out for snappers,' warned E.J.

The water was clouded with mud. We wouldn't see a snapper until we trod on it. But given the choice between putting my foot into the mouth of a snapper turtle or facing a grizzly bear, I'd choose the snapper every time.

With E.J. riding on my back and Sally following close behind, I waded into the creek. The water got quite deep towards the middle. It lapped around my waist and must have come up even higher on Sally. Luckily, there was hardly any current. We made it across OK. But we didn't go ashore. A couple of metres from the bank, I veered right and began wading upstream towards a thick stand of reeds growing in the creek like a small island. It looked like a good place to hide. There would be no scent trail for the grizzly to follow. Pushing our way into the middle of the reeds, we sank down to our chins in the cool brown water and waited.

Ten seconds later, I heard a snuffling sound. Moving really quietly for something so large, the grizzly came stalking down to the creek exactly where we'd entered the water. It paused and sniffed the air. We were downwind – it couldn't smell us. After a moment's hesitation, the huge bear stepped into the creek and ploughed across. Climbing the far bank, it shook itself like a giant dog, then disappeared into the rushes.

'Phew!' Sally breathed.

'That was close,' muttered E.J.

'Shhhhh,' I whispered.

With just our heads above the water, we stayed absolutely still in our swampy hiding place. It was lucky we did. Because after about a minute, the grizzly returned. It came right down to the creek's edge, sniffing the rushes, sniffing the air, sniffing the ground. Crossing back to the other side, the grizzly sniffed the bank where we'd entered the water. Then it sat down in the creek and looked back over its shoulder. There was a puzzled expression in its eyes, as if it was wondering where we'd got to.

Snuff, snuff, snuff, went its big wet nostrils.

A mosquito buzzed around my head, then settled on the side of my nose. It was right next to my left eye, but I didn't move a muscle. I let it have a free drink. The grizzly was only about six metres away. We were hidden in the reeds, but the slightest movement would attract its attention.

Hic! went Sally beside me. What a time to get the hiccups again! She raised one hand slowly out of the water and clamped it across her mouth. But it wasn't enough to completely muffle the sound.

Hic!

The bear turned its head in our direction.

Please don't let it see us! I prayed.

Hic!

The grizzly tilted its head to one side, listening. It was so close I could see little insects, no bigger than sandflies, darting about in its fur. I sank down in the water, trying to make myself smaller, trying to disappear, until only my eyes and the top of my head poked out of the creek and I could no longer breathe. On either side of me, Sally and E.J. did the same. We were three terrified kids trying to make ourselves invisible. Trying not to become bear food.

But it was too late. The grizzly was looking right at us. Its little piggy eyes locked with mine. Lifting its upper lip, it bared its teeth and made a loud blowing sound. Then it rose up on its hind legs, water pouring out of its fur, and let out a fearsome roar, halfway between the bark of a dog and the bellow of a bull.

We were dead meat.

14
COME AND
GET ME!

A strange thing happened. Instead of charging, the grizzly whipped its head around and snapped at the air. *Chomp!* Then it swung a huge forepaw, like someone swatting flies. *Swish!* But there weren't any flies, as far as I could see.

Chomp! went the bear's jaws again, closing on nothing.

Weird, I thought. It was fighting off imaginary flies.

Then another thought popped into my mind. Unless . . .

Something bounced off the grizzly's ear and came flying in our direction. I got a clear view of it before it plopped into the water. It was small and brown and shaped like an egg.

My hunch was right. Bigfoot or Cave Boy was hurling acorns again. Whoever it was, they were deadly accurate. *Pow! Pow! Pow!* Every acorn was right on target.

The bear soon got sick of being pelted with acorns. Letting out another bellow of rage, it thundered up the bank in the direction the acorns were coming from.

Look out, acorn-thrower, I thought.

As soon as the grizzly disappeared, E.J. sprang upright in the reeds beside me. 'We're outta here!' he cried. He took one step, let out a yelp of pain and fell face down in the water with a big splash.

For a terrible moment, I thought another snapper had got him. Then I remembered his foot. After our close encounter with the grizzly, E.J. must have forgotten about it, too. Until he'd tried to walk.

Sally helped E.J. climb onto my back, then we waded ashore on the opposite side of the creek to where the grizzly had disappeared. I looked back, but I couldn't see any sign of the bear, or anyone else. Whoever threw the acorns had saved our lives.

Cold and dripping wet, we continued following the creek bank in the direction of the farm.

At least, I *hoped* that was the direction we were going. Ever since we'd arrived at the creek, I'd been worried we'd lost our way. Where was the wide, stony river I'd seen from up near the road? The river that led to the farm? All we could do was follow the creek and hope that sooner or later it would lead us there.

'Do you think it'll come after us?' Sally asked, looking over her shoulder.

'The grizzly or Bigfoot?' said E.J.

'Both, I guess.'

I struggled along under E.J.'s weight. 'Was it the same grizzly?' I asked, already puffed even though we'd only been walking for a few minutes.

'Sure looked like the same one,' E.J. said. 'Did you see the way it was following our scent?'

I shivered. And not just because of my wet clothes. It's the creepiest feeling when you're out in the wild and things want to eat you.

'Do grizzlies often go after people?' asked Sally.

'Usually only when you get too close to them,' E.J.

said. 'But sometimes you get a mean old bear that attacks people for no reason.'

Suddenly I thought of a reason. It was the same reason the black bear had kept trying to get into the bus after our crash. Raspberry cordial.

I'd rolled in the spilled cordial when I was getting Mr Johnson out.

'Let's stop for a second,' I said.

After E.J. slid off my back, I unbuttoned my shirt and looked at the shoulder where I'd come in contact with the cordial. There was a pale pink stain. The creek water had washed most of it out. But not all of it. When I raised the shirt to my nose, there was still a faint whiff of raspberries. I'd left a smear of the sweet scent on every leaf and bush and branch I'd rubbed against on my way down the hill. It was probably in the air as well. To the grizzly, with its super-powerful nose, it was an irresistible invitation. *Come and get me!*

Not any more. I rolled my shirt into a ball and tossed it into the creek.

'Now try to track us, Mr Grizzly,' I said.

E.J. was wearing a T-shirt under his scout top.

He lent it to me. I was much bigger than him, so it was a tight fit. But it was better than nothing. The mosquitoes were getting bad. The T-shirt had a cartoon moose on the front. *Welcome to Rainbow Lake,* it said underneath.

I didn't know where Rainbow Lake was, but I wished I was there right now. Then I felt selfish for thinking that. I was Baloo, and people were depending on me. Lives were at stake. This wasn't a time for daydreams about being somewhere else.

This was a time for action.

14
WHAM!

Just as I'd hoped, the creek led us to the river. Now all we had to do was follow it downsteam to the farm.

Soon help would be on its way for E.J.'s dad, Will, Mum and the other four cubs we'd left behind.

I put E.J. down so we could drink from a small, crystal-clear pool at the river's edge.

'Look!' Sally pointed across the river. 'A badger.'

A cute-looking animal had emerged from the forest on the other side. It looked like an overgrown possum, with a fat stripy tail and black markings around its eyes.

'That's not a badger,' E.J. said. 'It's a raccoon.'

We watched it come trotting across the stony

riverbank towards the water. It stopped when it saw us and sat down on its haunches.

'We won't hurt you, raccoon,' Sally said softly.

After checking us out for a few seconds, the raccoon seemed to decide that we weren't a threat. It came right to the water's edge and jumped onto a small pointy rock about 20 centimetres from shore. It teetered there for a second, being very careful to keep its paws clear of the water, then hopped across to another rock. When that rock wobbled, it jumped to the next one. It was crossing the river, using the rocks as stepping stones. Coming straight towards us.

'What's it doing?' I asked.

'Dunno,' said E.J., wobbling on one foot as he tried to stand up.

Sally, who was closest to the approaching raccoon, started backing away.

'It's scaring me,' she said.

It was making me nervous, too. I didn't know much about raccoons, but this wasn't how wild animals were supposed to behave. Unless they were dangerous.

I bent and picked up a stone.

E.J. leaned against a boulder, holding his injured foot clear of the ground as he watched the raccoon scrambling across the rocks towards us.

'Oh no!' he muttered. 'I think it's got rabies.'

I knew about rabies. It's a really nasty disease. If animals get it, they go crazy. They attack anything – other animals, trees, even people. And if they bite a person, they can get rabies, too. People can die from it.

'*RUN, SALLY!*' I yelled.

My warning came too late. Sally was still going backwards. The raccoon reached dry land and darted at her so fast, she didn't have time to turn and run.

But I had time to throw my stone.

The raccoon was too quick. It saw the stone coming and jumped high into the air. The stone flew under its belly and nearly hit Sally on the foot.

'Sorry,' I said, stooping to pick up another stone.

'*LOOK OUT!*' yelled E.J.

The raccoon had twisted around in mid-air. It hit the ground running.

Straight at me.

I was stooped over, legs bent, in the act of picking

90

up the second stone. There wasn't time to straighten up. The raccoon came at me like a furry missile.

My last view of the raccoon was its pink drooling mouth getting bigger, bigger, BIGGER.

WHAM!

I didn't see what happened next. Sally and E.J. described it later. But they didn't see much, either. One moment they were watching the raccoon fly towards me, the next a wolf came out of nowhere.

The raccoon never knew what hit it.

By the time I'd straightened up and looked around, the big grey wolf was bounding back towards the trees, shaking the raccoon's limp body in its powerful jaws. Eight or nine other wolves came to meet it. For a few seconds there was a savage tug of war as the wolf pack fought over their prize. Then a low whistle came from the forest. At once, the wolves dropped the dead raccoon and melted back into the trees.

'Man, oh man!' breathed E.J. Raising one hand, he measured a distance of about one centimetre between his thumb and forefinger. 'That wolf came *this* close to taking your head off!'

'I don't think it was after Baloo,' Sally said.

E.J. gave a nervous laugh. 'Of course it wasn't after him. He'd be dead if it was.'

Like the raccoon, I thought. I almost felt sorry for it. But the wolf had done it a favour – saved it from a slow, agonising death from rabies. I hoped the wolf wouldn't catch the disease.

'That's twice I've been saved by wolves,' I said, staring into the forest where they'd disappeared. 'And once by flying acorns. It's almost as if someone's looking after us.'

'You mean like God?' said Sally.

'No, the person who called the wolves off.'

'What person?'

'Didn't you hear someone whistle?'

Sally and E.J. shook their heads.

'Could have been a bird,' E.J. said.

I shrugged. E.J. might be right. It made more sense than someone whistling. The wolves probably dropped the raccoon because they realised it was diseased, not because someone called them off. The whistle was just a bird.

But birds don't throw acorns, said the little voice in my head.

16
SURROUNDED
BY WOLVES

Something was following us. I kept hearing rustling noises in the forest at the edge of the river. But every time we stopped to rest, the noises stopped, too.

I didn't say anything to E.J. and Sally, in case it was just my imagination playing tricks on me. We were nearly at the farm. Our troubles would soon be over, and help would be on its way for Mum and the others.

'Yikes!' said Sally.

Fifty metres ahead, a monkey-like figure came scampering out of the forest on all fours. It stopped next to the river and stood semi-upright, facing us.

We stopped, too.

'Is it Bigfoot's kid?' asked E.J.

I nodded, even though I wasn't sure about the Bigfoot part. I still thought of him as Cave Boy. 'I think he's waiting for us.'

Sally dropped behind me as I walked slowly forward, piggybacking E.J. When we got close to him, the boy sank into a crouch. He looked ready to run.

'He's scared,' E.J. whispered.

I felt scared, too. Dressed in ragged pelts and crouching on all fours, the boy looked more like a wild animal than a human.

'Hello,' I said, trying to sound friendly.

Cave Boy licked his lips, making a strange whimpering noise. Suddenly he darted forward and crouched at my feet. His whole body was shaking.

'It's OK,' I said. 'We're not going to hurt you.'

The boy didn't move, just crouched there, looking up at me. There was a pleading look in his big brown eyes.

'I think he wants you to pat him,' Sally whispered.

I nearly laughed. 'He isn't a dog!'

'He's acting like one,' she said.

'More like a puppy,' said E.J.

Suddenly I got it. He *was* acting like a puppy. Bringing one arm out from under E.J.'s knee, I reached down and nervously patted Cave Boy's head. He licked my hand.

'Eeeew!' said E.J.

'Remember what you said about Mowgli in *The Jungle Book*,' I said to Sally. 'I think Cave Boy's the same – he's been brought up by wolves.'

'Cool!' she said.

I kept patting him. He was no longer shaking, but his eyes still had a questioning look. He wanted something, but he couldn't tell me what it was.

'*Mwaa mwaa*,' he said softly.

'What's *mwaa mwaa*?' I asked.

Cave Boy nodded. '*Mwaa mwaa!*' he repeated, louder this time. He pointed across the river.

All we could see over there was forest.

'I don't know what *mwaa mwaa* is,' I said.

Cave Boy straightened up and turned towards the river. He made a beckoning gesture. '*Mwaa mwaa*,' he said, stepping lightly from rock to rock like the raccoon had done.

'Does he want us to follow him?' asked Sally.

'Let's find out,' I said.

E.J. pulled against my shoulders, like a rider slowing his horse. 'No, Baloo. We've got to go to the farm and get help for Dad and the others.'

He was right. I was Baloo, and I had a job to do. Cave Boy would have to wait. He'd reached the far side of the river and stood watching us.

'*Mwaa mwaa*!' he called, urgently beckoning at us to cross.

'Sorry! We have to go to the farm!' I shouted, even though I knew he couldn't understand a word I was saying.

But he understood we weren't going to help him. Raising one hand to his lips, Cave Boy let out a piercing whistle.

'Yikes!' said Sally.

We were surrounded by wolves.

17
MWAA MWAA

They were the same wolves that had come to our aid twice before. But this time they looked anything but friendly. Snarling and bristling, the huge yellow-eyed wolves closed in on us from all sides.

'Stay close to me,' I said softly.

With E.J. on my back and Sally clutching my elbow, we backed down to the river and started wobbling across the rocks towards Cave Boy on the other side.

The wolves stood in a line at the water's edge, watching us go.

Cave Boy waited until we had staggered ashore, then put two fingers to his mouth and whistled again. Like well-trained sheepdogs, the wolves turned and went trotting away into the trees.

'*Mwaa mwaa*,' said Cave Boy, leading us towards the forest.

I badly needed a rest – E.J. was getting heavy – but I was too scared to stop. One whistle from Cave Boy would bring the wolves running.

'He *is* just like Mowgli,' Sally whispered.

'There's one difference,' said E.J. 'Mowgli was a good guy.'

'I wouldn't call Cave Boy a bad guy,' I said.

'How do you figure that?'

'He got the wolves to chase the grizzly away when we were up the hill,' I said. 'He saved us from the raccoon. He threw acorns at the grizzly.'

'Hang on,' said E.J. 'If Cave Boy was the one throwing acorns, then he threw them at us, too.'

'It might have been a warning,' I said. 'To make us hurry because he knew the grizzly was coming after us.'

'Speaking of the grizzly . . .' Sally said in a terrified whisper.

I looked over my shoulder.

Shishkebab!

A huge brown bear was coming along the bank on the opposite side of the river. One look was enough to tell me that it was the same grizzly that had been following us all afternoon.

Would it *ever* give up?

'I don't think it saw us,' Sally breathed as we entered the trees.

'It doesn't need to see us,' said E.J. 'It just needs to *smell* us.'

'But I threw my shirt away,' I said. 'I don't smell like raspberry cordial any more.'

'Yes, you do,' E.J. said. He was riding on my back and his nose was just above my head. 'It's in your hair.'

'You should have said something!'

'I didn't notice till a couple of minutes ago, when we were surrounded by wolves. And I figured the wolves were going to kill us anyway.'

I stopped in my tracks. I'd had an idea.

'Why have we stopped?' Sally whispered.

I explained my idea. 'If we stop following Cave Boy, then he'll call the wolves again.'

'Isn't that the *last* thing we want?' said E.J., sliding down off my back to give me a break.

I shook my head. 'The last thing we want is the grizzly to catch us. If Cave Boy calls the wolves, they might chase the bear away like they did last time.'

It seemed like a good idea, but there was one problem. Cave Boy had gone on ahead. He didn't know we'd stopped.

With every passing second, the grizzly was getting closer.

'Let's see where Cave Boy is,' I said nervously.

There was no track to follow but we soon caught up with him. He was coming back through the forest towards us. Before I could do my stopping thing again, I glimpsed something through a gap in the trees behind him. A fence. There was a gate in the fence and a wide grassy paddock on the other side.

Cave Boy had led us to the farm!

He seemed really excited. Running to meet us, he grabbed my wrist.

'*Mwaa mwaa*!' he said, tugging me forward.

But instead of leading me to the gate, Cave Boy took

me to a small gully, choked with brambles, just inside the forest's fringe. On the opposite side of the gully, a big corrugated iron cylinder lay on its side under some trees. It had a tiny opening at one end, covered in heavy wire mesh, like the window of a prison cell. There was a sliding door at the other end, and some cables running across the top.

'It's a bear trap,' E.J. said.

Cave Boy released my hand. '*Mwaa mwaa*!' he cried, racing ahead.

As we followed Cave Boy through the brambles, E.J. explained that traps like these were set by national park rangers to capture bears that were causing trouble on farms or in towns. The traps were baited with meat. When a bear went in and tried to drag the meat out, a hidden wire sprung the door catch, trapping the bear inside. The captured animal was then taken to a place where there weren't humans.

'There's something inside it,' Sally whispered.

'That's all we need,' muttered E.J. 'Another bear.'

Cave Boy got to the trap ahead of us. He pressed his face and hands against the mesh-covered window. A long pink tongue licked his nose and fingers.

'Eeeew!' said Sally.

'I don't think it's a bear,' I said as we cautiously approached.

There was a savage growl from inside the trap when the animal saw us. E.J. slid down from my back.

'Sounds like a wolf,' he said, hopping over for a closer look.

Cave Boy was talking softly through the thick steel mesh. *'Mwaa mwaa. Mwaa mwaa.'*

Suddenly I got it. *'Mwaa mwaa* means mama. The wolf's his mother!'

'But it's a wolf,' E.J. said, looking in.

'He thinks he's a wolf, too,' I said. 'This must be the mother wolf that looked after him when he was little.'

Cave Boy turned from the window and took hold of my wrist again. He led me to the other end of the trap, where the reinforced steel door was. He rattled the door, then looked at me and made a whimpering noise.

At last everything made sense. Cave Boy's mother had become caught in the bear trap, and neither he nor the other wolves could get her out. That's why he'd led us here, and why he and the pack had protected us – so we could release her.

'Sally, give me a hand to get this open,' I called.

E.J. hopped around to help, too. We slid our fingers under the door and heaved. It was heavy. There was a squealing sound. Slowly the door slid upwards in its metal frame. Then – *click* – a spring-loaded catch locked into place, holding the door open.

The mother wolf cowered down the other end of the trap, her yellow eyes glinting in the semi-darkness. She was afraid to come out while E.J., Sally and I stood at the entrance.

'OK, guys, let's make room for her,' I whispered.

Sally and I moved aside, but E.J. stayed where he was.

'E.J., get away from the door,' I said.

He wasn't listening. His eyes were on Cave Boy as he disappeared into the trap to coax his mother out.

CLANG!

'Holy guacamole!' I gasped.

E.J. had released the catch and the door had slammed shut, trapping Cave Boy inside with his mother.

'We're rich!' E.J. said with a triumphant grin.

18
HUMUNGUS

'Let him out!' cried Sally.

E.J. leaned against the door of the trap. 'No way, José. If he's that orphan boy who disappeared, there are 50,000 reasons why I'm not letting him out.'

'Who cares about a stupid reward?' Sally growled.

E.J. shrugged. 'It's not only about the reward,' he said. 'We'll be doing him a favour. He belongs with people, not with wolves.'

Sally looked at me for support. 'Make E.J. let him go, Baloo. It isn't fair to trick him after he saved us all those times.'

I didn't think it was fair, either. But E.J. had a good

point. Cave Boy was a human, not a wild animal.

'Maybe we – '

Before I could finish what I was going to say, two things happened.

One: there was a blowing noise, *whuff, whuff, whuff*, from somewhere in the brambles.

Two: Cave Boy let out a long, piercing whistle.

'Let's get out of here!' I said.

Loading E.J. onto my back, I headed along the top of the gully towards the fence in a bent-over, stumbling run. Sally jogged beside me. I was slowing her down. *Go ahead*, I wanted to say. *Get help*. But talking might have attracted the grizzly's attention. It had sounded really close.

We reached the fence and followed it until we came to the gate. While Sally struggled with the catch, I had a quick look over my shoulder. I half-expected to see a huge brown bear lumbering through the trees towards us, but the coast was clear. The grizzly must have gone the other way around the brambles, distracted by Cave Boy's shrill whistles.

He was still whistling. Still calling the rest of the

wolves. Would they hear him? And if they did hear, would they attack the grizzly, or come after us?

Sally dragged the gate open. We slipped through into the paddock and she closed it behind us. Yaaay! We'd reached the farm.

But we were far from safe. A wooden gate and a rickety fence were all that stood between us and the forest. They were hardly going to stop a 300-kilogram grizzly.

E.J. must have been reading my thoughts. 'Giddy-up,' he whispered.

I didn't need any encouragement. We set off across the paddock like a horse and rider. A very slow and tired horse.

'Run ahead, Sally,' I puffed. It was safe to talk now – we were 100 metres from the forest's edge. 'Get to the farmhouse and tell them what's happened.'

'Where is it?' she asked.

'I don't know. Maybe over the next rise.'

Sally went racing ahead. When she'd said she was a good runner, she hadn't been kidding. She reached the top of the rise way ahead of us. Another fence ran along the skyline. Sally climbed across it and disappeared over the crest, still running like a human greyhound.

The human horse wasn't doing so well. I was pooped. I slowed to a walk. E.J. leaned forward and put his mouth next to my ear.

'Giddy-up!' he said.

I stopped. He was really pushing his luck. 'If you say that one more time, E.J., I'm putting you down and you can crawl the rest of the way on your hands and knees!'

'Sorry,' he said. 'It's just that we've got company.'

Uh oh. With a sinking feeling in the pit of my stomach, I turned around and looked back the way we'd come.

A hundred and fifty metres away, a big dark shape stood at the edge of the shadowy forest, peering though the fading daylight in our direction.

'Do you think it can see us?' I whispered.

'Who knows,' E.J. said as the grizzly advanced slowly towards the gate, its nose to the ground like a giant tracker dog. 'But it sure as eggs can smell us.'

This time there was nowhere to hide. No wolves to help us. No Cave Boy throwing acorns.

E.J. and I were on our own.

But not for long. When we got to the top of the hill, we met Sally coming the other way. She vaulted the fence separating our paddock from the next one, then doubled over like she'd just run a marathon. Her shoulders heaved as she gasped for breath.

'Sally, what's wrong?' I asked.

She pointed back the way she'd come. 'Something's coming,' she panted. 'It's humungous!'

19
TIME TO RUN!

There was a thunder of hooves. The ground shook. A black silhouette came galloping towards the fence. It was as tall as a horse and as broad as a bull, and its massive woolly head was bigger than a lion's. A lion with horns! I thought the charging monster was going to smash through the fence, but it stopped at the very last moment.

'It's a bison,' E.J. said.

Bison are the largest land animals in North America. Adult bulls can weigh up to a tonne and stand two metres tall. No wonder Sally had been in such a hurry to cross the fence.

But we were in a hurry to cross the fence, too.

Going the other way.

I looked over my shoulder. Down near the other fence, the grizzly was standing on its hind legs, pushing against the gate.

'Are bison dangerous?' I asked.

'Dunno,' said E.J.

There was a crack of splintering wood in the distance and the gate fell flat on the ground. The grizzly came barging through the gap.

There's a saying my dad uses – caught between a rock and a hard place. That was us. In our paddock was the grizzly, in the next paddock was the bison.

'*HEEEEEELP!*' yelled Sally.

'Shhhhh!' I hissed. 'No one's going to hear you except the grizzly.'

'They might hear at the house,' she argued.

'You saw the house?' I asked.

She nodded. 'It's just over the hill. I nearly got there, but the bison chased me back.'

That decided it. If the house was just over the hill, that's where we were going.

I slid E.J. off my back and approached the fence.

I had never heard of anyone being killed by a bison, but lots of people got killed by grizzlies. Taking a deep breath, I climbed across the fence onto the bison's side. It backed away from me.

'You next, Sally,' I whispered.

After Sally had climbed over, I parted the two bottom wires to allow E.J. to crawl through. Then I turned and faced the bison again, so E.J. could climb onto my back. The bison snorted and pawed the ground. Then it lowered its huge head and butted me in the chest, sandwiching me and E.J. against the fence. The wires creaked.

There was another noise, too – the *huff, huff, huff* of a running bear. It was growing louder every moment. But I couldn't look round to see how close it was. I couldn't move. Neither could E.J. A thousand kilograms of aggro bison had us pinned to the fence.

All sorts of things rushed through my mind at that moment. Mum had sent me to get help and now I was going to die. E.J. was going to die. His father would probably die, too, because how was he going to get to hospital now? And what about Mum and Will and the other cubs? What would happen to them?

The one person I *didn't* think about was Sally.

Suddenly the bison gave an angry snort and whirled around. Free to move at last, I staggered away from the fence, lost my balance and fell flat on the ground. E.J. landed on top of me. The bison's hooves thumped past, showering us with dirt. A small figure in a cub's uniform was hanging onto its tail, being dragged through the grass.

Go, Sally! I thought. She must have run around behind the hulking animal and yanked its tail when she saw that E.J. and I were in trouble.

But now she was the one in trouble. The bison turned in a circle, swinging its horns. Sally let go just in time. She tried to roll out of the way, but the fence blocked her escape. The huge beast turned and faced her. It bellowed and pawed the ground, sending clods of earth flying into the air.

Then I saw something behind Sally. Something worse than the bison.

'*GRIZZLY!*' I yelled.

Sally screamed and covered her head as the huge bear came bounding towards the fence. It tried to jump over, but it hit the top wire. A section of fence collapsed to the ground. Sally was caught underneath. The grizzly landed right beside her. It sniffed her lifeless form, then turned towards E.J. and me, lying frozen in terror only a few metres away.

It licked its lips.

A bison wouldn't normally attack a grizzly bear. It would be more likely to run away. But this bison was angry. It didn't like having its tail pulled and it was ready to take on anything.

WHOMP!

One thousand kilograms versus 300 kilograms. It wasn't an even contest. But the grizzly is the most ferocious of all bears. No North American animal could beat it in a one-to-one scrap. Even though the bison lifted it high into the air, the bear held on with its front legs wrapped around the larger animal's neck. The bison staggered away from the flattened fence – and away from Sally, E.J. and me – swinging the grizzly back and forth. It was a battle of the giants. In the fading light, they looked like a single animal, a strange mythical creature with multiple legs and two heads.

Sally was still lying under the collapsed fence.

She wasn't moving. I crawled over to her, terrified by what I might find. It seemed impossible that she could have survived. But her eyes swivelled round when I approached.

'Help me, Baloo,' she gasped. 'I'm stuck.'

The stumps of two broken fence posts poked out of the ground, one on either side of her, like the pylons of a suspension bridge. They'd held the tangle of wires just high enough off the ground to stop Sally from being crushed by the grizzly when it had flattened the fence. But now they were holding her down. I heaved the wires up and Sally wriggled free.

'Are you hurt?'

'No,' she said, watching the fight.

The two animals were 30 metres away. The bison had shaken the grizzly free. They were circling each other like a pair of heavyweight boxers.

'Let's get out of here before they notice us,' I whispered.

Hoisting E.J. onto my back, I followed Sally over the crest of the hill.

And there, nestled among a sprawling fruit orchard,

was the farmhouse.

My legs were shaking from the strain of carrying E.J. all afternoon, but I hardly noticed the pain as we staggered down the long slope towards the house. We were nearly there. Nearly at the end of our journey. Just another 150 metres.

Yet when I looked at the house, I had a strange feeling something was wrong. But I couldn't think what it was.

We crossed another fence and made our way through an orchard. The trees were planted in straight rows with furrows running between them. I had to be careful not to trip. There was another fence. This time we found a small gate. Sally opened it for me and E.J., then closed it behind us. There were shadowy rose bushes, a stretch of lawn, and a big horse trailer sitting at the side of a white circular driveway. My feet crunched across the gravel towards the house. An automatic sensor light came on, illuminating a wide veranda and children's toys scattered about. After everything we'd been through, it felt like a dream to be walking up someone's front steps. E.J. slid off my back, and I stretched my aching muscles.

Sally pressed the doorbell. We heard a *ding-dong* inside the house and stood back, waiting for someone to open the door. But nobody came. Sally pressed the button again. Apart from the noise of the doorbell, there was nothing but silence. I realised what had seemed strange about the house as we'd come down the hill. Even though it was getting dark, there were no lights showing through any of its windows.

'I don't think anyone's home,' I said.

Sally pressed the bell again, just to be sure. But nobody came to the door.

'What do we do now?' asked E.J.

I turned around. There was a barn on the other side of the yard and several smaller sheds.

'ANYBODY HOME?' I yelled.

My shout brought a reaction, but not the one I'd hoped for. A clink of chains, followed by loud barking. Over by the sheds, lit up by the sensor light, were two dog kennels. A pair of black-and-white farm dogs jumped and strained at the end of their chains.

'It's lucky they're tied up,' Sally said.

There was a pause in the barking and I heard another

sound. A deep, throaty growl. Slowly, I turned my head. Another dog stood at the corner of the veranda. It was half in the shadows, but I could see its teeth quite clearly. They were big. They were white. They were bared.

It wasn't pleased to see us.

'Go slowly down the steps,' I said to Sally. 'Whatever you do, don't run.

The dog edged forward into the light. It was a Doberman.

'E.J.?' I whispered.

'Yeah?' he answered, right behind me.

'Climb on my back.'

I stooped to make it easier. My head was almost level with the Doberman's. It growled again, a low, threatening rumble, and came stalking along the veranda with its ears back and its teeth showing.

I took a step backwards and nearly tripped on a child's tricycle. Stay calm, I told myself. The worst thing I could do was run. With E.J. on my back, I wouldn't even get to the stairs. The best plan was to stay still. The dog's owners had left it off its chain while they weren't home, so it probably wasn't dangerous.

'Good dog,' I said.

My words had a startling effect. The Doberman seemed to freeze. Its teeth disappeared inside its lips, it stopped growling, and it cowered at my feet, almost like Cave Boy had done when we first met him by the river. Then it turned, its claws skidding on the veranda boards, and shot back around the corner of the house.

'Have I got bad breath or something?' I joked.

E.J. laughed, but Sally didn't. She was standing at the foot of the stairs, looking the other way. In the same direction the Doberman had been facing before it took off.

'Yikes!' she whispered.

E.J. and I turned our heads. A huge dark shape came lumbering through the rose bushes from the direction of the orchard.

The grizzly.

Now it was time to run!

20
TOBY'S LIMO

'Quick!' I hissed.

Sally didn't need to be told – she was already back at the top of the stairs. We raced along the veranda and around the corner. Past a small plastic swing set. Past an outdoor table and some chairs. Around another corner. When we got to the back door, we didn't even bother knocking. Sally tried the handle.

'Locked!' she breathed.

'What'll we do?' E.J. whispered.

I had an idea.

'The barn!' I said.

But there was one major problem with my idea. The

barn was round the front of the house and so was the grizzly.

Or was it?

I held my breath and listened. The chained dogs had stopped barking. What did that mean?

A board creaked just around the corner ahead of us. Next came the sound of skidding claws and the Doberman went flying past.

Clever grizzly. It was coming around the house in the opposite direction to us.

'Back the other way!' I hissed.

We went racing back the way we'd come. The chained dogs started barking again as soon as we came into view. Behind them was the barn, a bulky square shape against the evening sky.

Bent forward under E.J.'s weight, I staggered down the steps behind Sally. We crunched across the gravel towards the barn. The dogs were going crazy. I thought it was because of us. Then I heard another sound – *whuff, whuff, whuff*. Uh oh. I glanced over my shoulder. The grizzly came lumbering along the veranda, knocking the tricycle flying. It leapt down the steps in a single bound.

We weren't going to make it to the barn.

The horse trailer stood at the edge of the driveway. *Toby's Limo*, it said on the side. The door was wide open.

'In there!' I puffed, swerving up the ramp.

Sally shot in ahead of me.

E.J. grabbed the door as we went past and swung it closed behind us.

BANG!

A split second later there was an even louder bang as the grizzly hit the door from the outside. The trailer rocked on its springs.

'That was close!' gasped E.J.

But the danger wasn't over yet. The door latch had to be worked from outside, so we couldn't lock ourselves in. All we could do was hang onto the iron framework on the back of the door to stop it coming open while the grizzly tried to bite and claw its way in. Luckily, the enormously strong bear hadn't worked out that it had to pull the door to get it open, not push it.

After a few minutes, the grizzly gave up and tried to find another way in. *Toby's Limo* was fully enclosed, so it couldn't climb in over the top. But there was a

121

small window at the front for the horse (Toby?) to look out. When the grizzly looked *in*, we were plunged into complete darkness. None of us moved a muscle as it pressed its big furry head to the window. It tried to bite through the perspex, but the surface was too flat and smooth for its teeth to grip.

Finally, the grizzly returned to the door and began sniffing at the crack, only centimetres from our hands. At one point it stuck its claws in. Realising the danger, we all pulled hard on the door frame and the bear's claws got stuck. With a snort of anger, the grizzly tugged itself free. It snuffled around outside for a while, then we heard it softly crunching away across the driveway.

We waited about ten minutes, not talking and hardly even daring to breathe. *Toby's Limo* smelt of hay and another smell that I recognised from my grandparents' farm in Australia. It was a cattle smell. Maybe Toby was a bull?

It was silent outside. The dogs had stopped barking. I tiptoed to the front of the trailer and peered out the window. The sensor light at the house had gone off. I couldn't see anything except a few stars scattered across a patch of purple sky. I went back to join Sally and E.J. by the door.

'What are we going to do, Baloo?' Sally whispered.

I wished she wouldn't call me that – it made me feel like I should have all the answers to our problems, and I didn't.

'We'll wait here till the people come home,' I decided.

'What if they don't come home?' E.J. asked. 'What if they've gone away on vacation?'

'Their dogs are here,' I said. 'Nobody goes away and leaves their dogs to look after themselves.'

We were silent for a while. Someone's stomach rumbled. It was seven or eight hours since we'd eaten anything, but hunger was the least of our problems.

'I hope Dad's all right,' E.J. said softly.

I was worried about him, too. And about Mum and the others. It was so frustrating. We'd come all this way, survived so many dangers, and finally got to the farm – only to become trapped in a horse trailer. 'Akela will look after him. She used to be a nurse.'

'He should be in hospital,' E.J. said.

I knew he was right. Mum and Will probably needed

hospital treatment, too. But what could we do? The house was locked. Nobody was home. And the grizzly could be lurking anywhere, waiting for us to leave the trailer.

Suddenly there was a ringing sound.

'What's that?' asked Sally.

'A phone,' I said.

We listened to the phone ringing. It was loud.

'It's coming from the barn,' E.J. whispered.

Sally was on the other side of the trailer. 'No it isn't,' she said, pressing her ear to the wall. 'It's in the house.'

I cracked the door open a couple of centimetres and put my ear to the gap. They were both right. 'There are two phones,' I said. 'One in the barn, and one in the house. They must be on the same line.'

The ringing stopped.

'Too bad!' said E.J.

I knew what he was thinking. So near and yet so far. I made a decision. 'I'm going to look for the phone,' I said.

Sally gripped my arm. 'You can't, Baloo! The grizzly's out there.'

'The barn's close. I can get there in five seconds.'

E.J. gripped my other arm. 'Don't risk it, Sam.'

I shook myself free and rose to my feet. 'Akela sent me to get help,' I said, 'and that's what I'm going to do.'

'But the grizzly might be waiting,' whispered Sally.

'The barn might be locked,' said E.J.

'Close the door after me,' I told them, and slipped out into the night.

21
YIKES!

I was only two steps from the trailer when the sensor light snapped on, capturing me like a rabbit in headlights. Uh oh! So much for sneaking to the barn under the cover of darkness. I glanced over my shoulder.

The Doberman was halfway up the stairs. That's what had triggered the motion sensor. Behaving more like a frightened pup than a guard dog, it slunk off along the veranda and disappeared around the corner. That told me one thing – the grizzly wasn't up by the house.

So where was it?

The quicker I reached the safety of the barn, the better. But I had to be careful. If I was going flat out, and the grizzly came out of the shadows in front of me, I might literally run into it. So it was safer to walk rather than run, and keep my eyes peeled.

The sensor light threw my shadow ahead of me. When I crept past the chained dogs, I didn't hear a peep out of them. They were hiding at the back of their kennels – not from me, but from the grizzly. Wherever it was.

E.J. had been worried that the barn might be locked, but the door was wide open, gaping like a huge black mouth in the front of the building. It gave me a really bad feeling.

What if the grizzly's inside the barn? asked the little voice in my head.

At that moment, the sensor light went off. Suddenly, I could no longer see the barn, much less inside it.

I nearly chickened out. Nearly turned around and raced back to the trailer. E.J. and Sally wouldn't blame me. Neither would Mum. She'd sent me to get help, not to get killed. How many times in the past had she said to me, 'Don't take unnecessary risks, Sam'?

Somewhere inside the barn, the phone started ringing again. *Ring ring, ring ring.* It seemed to be calling me.

I took a deep breath and forced my feet to start walking. Into the gaping black mouth of the barn. It was so dark that I couldn't even see my hands stretched out in front of me. I was like a blind person, feeling my way ahead with my shuffling feet. The phone kept ringing. How long before they'd give up and think no one was home?

Get a move on, Sam! My outstretched hands brushed against a rough wooden pillar. I felt my way carefully past it, guided by the sound of the ringing phone. It grew louder and louder. I was really close. One of my knees bumped a chair, my hands fumbled across a bench.

Found it!

'Hello,' I gasped into the receiver.

There was a pause, then a woman's voice said, 'I'm sorry, I think I have the wrong number.'

'No, you've got the right number,' I cried. 'Don't hang up!' Then I told her who I was and what had happened.

The woman was the sister of the lady who lived on the farm. She sounded nice. 'I'll get help,' she said. 'You and your friends stay put. Lock yourselves in Toby's trailer until someone gets there.'

I thanked her and hung up. Because I was in a such panic about the grizzly, I'd forgotten to tell her about Mum and E.J.'s dad and the other cubs. What an idiot!

I picked up the phone again and tried to dial 000. It was really hard in the dark because the numbers didn't light up. Then I remembered where I was – the USA, not Australia – and that the emergency number was 911. That was even harder to dial in the dark than 000.

Another woman answered and I quickly told her what was going on.

'I need to know where the bus accident happened, Sam,' she said calmly.

I realised I didn't have a clue. 'I'd better get E.J.,' I said, feeling like even more of an idiot. 'Don't hang up.'

The woman promised to wait. It was a cordless phone, so I took it with me and started feeling my way back towards the open barn door. Because it was lighter outside than inside the barn, I could see the doorway ahead of me, a large pale rectangle with a scatter of twinkling stars at the top.

Something else was there. In the bottom half of the doorway. Coming towards me!

Shishkebab! The grizzly!

But a grizzly doesn't have two heads.

'Baloo?' said one of the heads.

'Sam?' said the other.

It was Sally and E.J. She was piggybacking him.

'I told you guys to stay in the trailer,' I growled, helping E.J. down off Sally's back.

'We got scared,' she puffed.

I remembered that she and E.J. were only nine years old. Who could blame them for being scared?

'We're going to be OK,' I said, quickly telling them about the phone calls. I handed the phone to E.J.

'Explain where the bus crashed,' I told him.

While E.J. described to the 911 woman where his father had turned off the highway, Sally and I dragged the barn door closed. Now I felt safe.

'See if you can find a light switch,' I whispered to Sally.

I began feeling along the wall near the door for a switch. My hand bumped against the curved steel prongs of a pitchfork. I grabbed it by the handle to stop it falling over.

'Found it!' said Sally.

I heard a small click. All along the rafters high above us, neon tubes sputtered into life. Next moment, the barn was filled with light.

'Yikes!' said Sally.

22
MOVIE POSTER

Here's a picture that's burned into my memory like a movie poster you've seen 100 times and will never forget.

The scene is the inside of a barn. There are big stainless-steel tanks and canning machinery along one side, and a kind of office on the other. Above the office, a shadowy loft runs the length of the building. It's stacked with cardboard boxes. A blue tractor is parked down the far end. Next to it is a yellow quad bike. Even though the lights are on, you can see it's night-time because of the shadows in the corners of the building, and the shadows cast by the people.

There are two people in the picture – a boy and a girl. The boy wears a cub uniform but he only has one shoe. He holds his bare foot just clear of the ground, and leans against the ladder leading up to the loft. He has a phone to his ear, and there's a startled look on his face, as if he's just seen a ghost. The girl wears a cub uniform, too. Her eyes are bulging like the boy's and her mouth is wide open. It looks like she's about to scream.

There's another person in the barn but you can't see him, only his shadow on the floor at the bottom of the picture, and the prongs of a pitchfork he's holding out in front of him like a weapon.

At the very centre of the barn, exactly where the pitchfork is pointing, stands a huge grizzly bear.

23
SHOWTIME!

The grizzly blinked its eyes as they adjusted to the sudden light. I reckoned we had about two seconds before it charged.

'Go up the ladder!' I cried.

E.J. dropped the phone and began awkwardly climbing the ladder, compensating for his injured foot by crabbing up the rungs on his right knee. But Sally hesitated. The grizzly was on the other side of the ladder. To reach the ladder, she'd have to run *towards* the bear.

So would I.

If someone made a list of the world's top ten scariest things, running towards a grizzly would be on it.

I rushed past Sally, and past the ladder. With the pitchfork extended like a six-pronged spear.

Attack is the best means of defence.

The grizzly saw me coming and reared up on its hind legs. It was huge. It looked about two-and-a-half metres tall. As I approached it, I slowed to a walk, waving the pitchfork back and forth.

'Sally, go up the ladder,' I said over my shoulder.

The grizzly dropped onto all fours and came to meet me. It moved warily, its eyes fixed on the sharp points of the pitchfork. I stopped and waited for it. The bear seemed to sense I didn't really want to take it on, and it grew in confidence. Suddenly it growled and took a swipe with one forepaw. My reaction was too slow. Before I could get the fork out of the way, one of its prongs buried itself deep into the pad of the bear's paw.

With a bellow of pain, the grizzly lurched backwards.

I took a quick look behind me. Sally was halfway up the ladder. E.J. was nowhere in sight. Despite his injured foot, he'd made it all the way up to the loft.

'Look out!' shrieked Sally.

It had been a mistake to look away from the bear.

Grizzlies are lightning fast. In the couple of seconds I'd been distracted, it hurled itself at me like a rugby player going for a head-high tackle. Head-high tackles are illegal. So are pitchforks used as weapons. I swung it in front of me in a jujitsu block.

CRACK!

The grizzly bit right through the handle, leaving me with half a pitchfork in each hand. Two weapons instead of one. But there wasn't time to use them. The grizzly was too big, too close and too fast. It had me cold.

Showtime!

But the grizzly hadn't counted on one thing – E.J.

Without warning, a big cardboard carton came flying down from the loft above us. It hit the grizzly on the neck, driving its head down almost to the floor. I whacked it with the pitchfork handle and jumped clear. The grizzly whirled around after me, swinging one paw in a vicious right hook. Its deadly claws caught the prongs of the stubby pitchfork and sent it flying across the barn. I was down to one weapon – the short length of handle. The grizzly bellowed like a bull and came at me again.

WHAP!

Another carton hit it on the head. This one exploded like a bomb. Cans flew everywhere. They rolled across the floor all around the grizzly. It was like trying to walk on marbles. The grizzly's feet went in four different directions. It collapsed in a big, furry heap.

I saw my chance. Before the bear had time to recover, I dropped the pitchfork handle, raced to the ladder and started climbing. Then something crashed into the ladder just below me. The world seemed to tip sideways. For a second, I thought the ladder was going to fall. But I kept climbing.

I could hear the grizzly huffing and snorting as it came up after me. The ladder swayed and creaked. The grizzly's hot breath warmed my heels. I saw Sally's face above me. She was holding the ladder steady with one hand, and reaching for me with the other. E.J. was there, too. Holding another carton.

'Duck your head, Sam!' he said.

I flattened myself against the ladder as the carton whizzed past, missing me by millimetres.

But it didn't miss the grizzly. There was a loud *CLUNK!* below me, and a bellow of rage.

I reached the top of the ladder and Sally helped me into the loft. E.J. came hopping over with another carton. He took aim and dropped it.

THUMP!

Poor bear, I thought. But I didn't really feel sorry for it. It had been chasing us all afternoon.

It was *still* chasing us. There was a creaking sound. The ladder started to rattle and shake. I looked over the edge. The grizzly was halfway up.

'Give me a hand, Sally,' I said.

We grabbed the top of the ladder and pushed. Almost in slow motion, the ladder started to tip backwards. Sensing what was about to happen, the grizzly climbed faster. For a moment its big, furry head was level with us. It clawed desperately at the edge of the loft, sending woodchips flying, as the ladder teetered on the point of balance. Then, with a roar of frustration, the grizzly disappeared.

CRASH!

I peered down after it. The grizzly was struggling out from under the wrecked ladder. Maybe it's had enough now, I thought. No such luck. The bear stood up, shook itself, then picked its way through the scattered cans towards the loft. It stopped directly beneath us and looked up. Even from eight metres away, its beady-eyed stare was enough to send a shiver down my spine.

'Do you think it can climb one of the wooden pillars?' Sally whispered.

I shook my head. 'I reckon we're safe now.'

Until I actually said it, I hadn't realised it was true. We *were* safe. Our adventure was over. We'd done what we had set out to do. We'd reached the farm and got help for E.J.'s dad and Mum and the rest of the Gunggari cub scouts. Finally I could relax.

But it's hard to relax when you're starving hungry.

'E.J., what's in those boxes you were throwing at the grizzly?'

He shrugged. 'Cans.'

'But what's in the cans?'

E.J. hopped over to a big stack of cartons. He broke one open and brought a can back.

'Hey, do you recognise this guy?' he said.

There was a bison's head on the label. It looked exactly like the one we'd met on our way across the farm. But what was written on the label was even more interesting.

TOBY'S FARM
Homemade Boysenberry Conserve

Now I knew who Toby was.

'What's conserve?' Sally asked.

'Jam,' I said, my mouth watering. The barn was a jam factory and the loft where we were trapped was the storage area. 'E.J., does your penknife have a tin-opener?'

We opened three cans and, using our fingers, began shovelling boysenberry jam into our mouths. Delicious!

'Someone's coming,' E.J. said with his mouth full.

He was right. I could hear a car. I paused, a handful of jam halfway to my mouth, wondering if it was the police, or maybe a park ranger with a dart gun to tranquilise the bear?

We listened to the crunch of wheels coming up the gravel driveway. They stopped. There was the sound of doors opening and closing. Then I heard children talking.

It must have been the family who lived in the house. Below us, the grizzly turned its broad, furry head in the direction of the voices.

'They should stay in the car,' E.J. whispered.

'They shouldn't even *be* here!' I said. 'I told the lady on the phone what was going on.'

We were all watching the grizzly now. It was standing up, facing the barn door. Luckily the door was closed.

'Maybe they haven't got a mobile phone,' said E.J. 'Or the battery's flat.'

Shishkebab!

'Then they don't know about the grizzly!' I said.

'Should we shout and warn them?' asked Sally.

Too late. The door rattled open and a man walked into the barn. He must have seen the lights and come to investigate.

'Holy smoke!' he muttered when he saw the broken cartons and the dented cans scattered all over the floor.

Then he noticed the grizzly, half-hidden in the shadows beneath the loft. He started backing towards the door.

Sally let out a gasp.

A little girl, about two years old, had followed the man into the barn. He didn't know she was there. He was about to trip over her.

'*LOOK OUT BEHIND YOU!*' I yelled.

But instead of looking behind him, the man looked up at me.

'What the –?!' he muttered.

The little girl looked up, too. She saw the three of us peering down from the loft and came trotting around the man's legs for a better view. He still hadn't seen her! And the girl hadn't seen the bear! Eyes screwed up against the glare of the overhead lights, she came toddling across the barn floor.

Straight towards the grizzly.

24
GRIZZLY TRAP

There was a rope and pulley at the far end of the loft, probably for hoisting the cartons up. Wiping my sticky hands on the front of my T-shirt, I ran to the rope and swung down to floor level. I landed right behind the bear. It swung its head around and looked at me with its small black eyes.

The little girl had seen it now and stood rooted to the spot in the middle of the barn, halfway between the bear and the man.

'Grab her!' I said, and started walking towards the grizzly.

I didn't have any plan other than distracting the bear

long enough for the man to rescue the little girl.

'C'MON, BEAR!' I shouted, waving my hands in the air.
'PICK ON SOMEONE YOUR OWN SIZE!'

The grizzly made a chuffing noise and turned to meet me. Behind it, the man was running towards the little girl.

'Cop this!' said E.J.

A can of Toby's Farm boysenberry conserve hit the grizzly on the shoulder. The huge angry bear spun around, snapping at the air, spit spraying from its jaws.

The man reached the little girl and picked her up.

Another can flew down. The grizzly batted it away like a tennis player.

The man was running towards the door with the little girl in his arms.

I started running, too. In the direction of the canning machinery on the other side of the barn. The grizzly came after me.

A jam tin bounced past me and clanged against one of the big stainless-steel tanks. I darted around the tank and squeezed through the gap between it and the wall. The grizzly was hot on my tail. I heard its chuffing breath as it pushed its head into the narrow gap. I was behind the jam-making machines now. There were pipes and hoses everywhere. I wormed my way further into the maze, then crouched in the tiny space behind a wide stainless-steel chute, hoping the grizzly was too big to follow.

For a few seconds nothing happened. My teeth rattled. My heart hammered. I tried not to breathe. Then I heard a slight noise right above me. I looked up and saw a big wet nose. The nostrils quivered, sniffing my scent – *whoof, whoof, whoof, whoof!* The grizzly had climbed across the machinery. It was forcing its way down between the chute and the wall.

I wriggled along the floor behind two big vats. From behind me came the scrape of claws on metal as the grizzly forced its way through. It was unstoppable!

I reached the end of the machinery and peered around a stack of wooden crates. The barn door was only a few metres away. Where was the grizzly? I could no longer hear it following me. Lying on the concrete halfway between me and the door was the prong-end half of the pitchfork.

Crawling out of my hiding place, I jumped to my feet and raced for the door. There was a clatter of toppling crates behind me and a familiar *chuff, chuff, chuff!*

From high in the loft, on the other side of the barn, came a loud scream:

'LOOK OUT BEHIND YOU, BALOO!'

I didn't need to look. I knew what was there. Three hundred kilos of charging grizzly. Lie down and cover my head? No way, E.J.!

Scooping up the pitchfork, I spun around and faced the bear. It was better to die fighting than to lie down and be eaten.

The grizzly's claws scraped across the concrete as it skidded to a halt. It had already been pricked by the pitchfork once, so now it was wary. Its eyes followed the fork's prongs as I waved them in its face.

I started backing towards the door. The grizzly followed. Its nostrils twitched and snuffled. *Why bother with my scent when I'm right here in front of you?* I thought.

My foot bumped one of the tins E.J. had thrown and suddenly I realised what the grizzly was sniffing. The jam I'd wiped on my T-shirt.

I glanced over my shoulder. We were nearly at the door. All the lights were on in the house. I hoped everyone was inside. The sensor light shone in my eyes, but I could see the outline of *Toby's Limo* halfway between the house and the barn.

Snuff, snuff, snuff! went the grizzly's nose as I led it out into the night.

'You've got a sweet tooth, haven't you?' I said.

I gently tapped its nose with the pitchfork. The grizzly squinted its eyes nearly all the way closed and drew back. It was facing the lights, relying more on its heightened sense of smell to know where I was, rather than its eyes.

Holding the fork in one hand, I quickly peeled the T-shirt over my head and free arm. Then I changed hands and yanked it all the way off.

Up at the house behind me, a door banged. The man shouted from the veranda: *'GET OUT OF THE WAY, SON, SO I CAN GET A CLEAR SHOT!'*

He was going to shoot the bear.

My hands were shaking as I jabbed the fork's spikes into the T-shirt. Then I dangled it in the bear's face.

'Follow me, if you want to live,' I said, and started backing in the direction of the house.

Once it got a close-up whiff of the jam, the grizzly didn't need any encouragement. Nose in the air, it came lumbering after the dangling T-shirt like an oversized puppy being offered a bone. But this was no puppy. One slip and I'd be dead. So would the grizzly. I could see the man standing at the top of the steps, aiming a rifle in our direction. But he couldn't shoot as long as I was in the way. I ran straight towards him, holding the pitchfork with E.J.'s T-shirt on it behind me. The grizzly was gaining speed. The faster I ran, the faster it ran. This was crazy!

'*WHAT ARE YOU DOING?*' yelled the man.

He soon found out. When I reached *Toby's Limo*, I rushed up the ramp as if I was going inside. The grizzly came rushing up after me. At the very last moment, I leapt sideways and tossed the pitchfork and T-shirt in through the open door. The grizzly brushed past me into the trailer, following the irresistible scent of the jam.

In two seconds flat I had the door closed and bolted, trapping the bear inside.

The man came walking down from the house carrying his rifle.

'That was the stupidest thing I've ever seen,' he said, checking that my grizzly trap was properly locked. Then he looked at me and smiled. 'And also the bravest.'

25
ROCKY

Mr Wakelin said it was 100 miles to the nearest hospital, so if E.J.'s foot wasn't hurting too much, would we mind spending the night at Toby's Farm and driving there tomorrow?

E.J.'s foot was wrapped in a bandage. 'It feels OK,' he said.

He, Sally and I were freshly showered and wearing clothes loaned to us by the Wakelins. Mine were too big, but it was nice to be dry and comfortable.

'Thanks for going to all this trouble, Mr Wakelin,' I said.

'Yeah, thanks,' said Sally.

We were all a bit distracted by what was happening

in the next room. Mrs Wakelin had just gone in there to answer the phone. We could only hear half of the conversation, but it sounded like the news we'd been anxiously waiting for.

She came back to the lounge room, grinning from ear to ear. 'That was the police,' she said. 'The emergency services have found the others.'

'How's Dad?' E.J. asked nervously.

'He's going to be fine. He's on his way to hospital right now in a rescue helicopter.'

'What about Will and my mum?' I asked.

'They're in the helicopter, too,' Mrs Wakelin said. 'Your mother wanted to pass on a message. I don't know what it means, but she said to tell you, "Baloo rules!"'

I laughed. 'Sally and E.J. rule, too,' I said.

Sally, E.J. and I exchanged high fives.

Mr Wakelin rubbed his hands together vigorously. 'Well, since it seems everyone's OK, let's go and eat!'

Mrs Wakelin and her eldest daughter, Helen, made a big stack of pancakes and heated up some Toby's Farm homemade maple sauce. The smell was enough to make you drool. We all squashed around the Wakelins' dining table. As well as Mr and Mrs Wakelin, there were their four daughters, whose ages ranged from about 12 down to two. Tyler, the youngest and the one I'd rescued, insisted on sitting next to me. Helen tried to sit on my other side, but Sally got there first.

'It must be nice to be so popular,' Mr Wakelin teased, and I felt my face turn red.

Mrs Wakelin smiled at me. 'Eat up, Sam. You must be famished.'

I *was* famished, but suddenly I couldn't eat. Neither could Sally. Across the table, E.J. was picking at his food, too.

'Hey, what's up with you guys?' Helen said. 'Don't you like our cooking?'

E.J. looked at me, then at Sally. We were all thinking the same thing. E.J. put his fork down. 'It doesn't seem right to be eating pancakes,' he said, 'when Cave Boy and his mother must be starving.'

'Who's Cave Boy?' asked Helen.

Fifteen minutes later, the Wakelins' big Jeep Cherokee four-wheel drive bumped across the flattened gate at the top end of their farm. Toby, the farm's mascot, had followed us part of the way down the hill from the broken fence, but then he'd turned around and gone galloping back to his paddock. Now we saw why. Several sets of eyes glowed in the headlights. They melted into the forest as we got nearer.

'Doggies!' said Tyler.

'They're wolves,' Helen corrected her.

Mr Wakelin stopped with the Jeep's headlights trained on the bear trap. He explained how the national parks service were trying to catch a troublesome grizzly, nicknamed Rocky, that had been raiding farms in the area for the past six months.

'Probably the same one you trapped in Toby's trailer, Sam. They're coming in the morning to take him to a national park up near Canada.' He paused and rubbed his chin. 'Maybe we should let them deal with this trap, too.'

'There's a boy in there,' Mrs Wakelin said.

'But there's a wolf, as well.'

'It won't hurt us,' I said, cracking my door open.

Everyone got out and cautiously approached the trap. Mr Wakelin carried his rifle. Mrs Wakelin had Tyler on

153

her hip, and the other three Wakelin girls followed her. Sally and I led the way, supporting E.J. between us as he hopped along on his good foot. We heard growling from inside the trap. Also a soft whimpering sound, like a puppy crying.

E.J. leaned close to me. 'Let him go, Sam,' he whispered. 'I don't want the reward money anymore.'

We'd been talking about it in the car. Mr Wakelin said it wasn't right for a boy to live with wolves. Mrs Wakelin said he was an orphan and the wolves were his family now. I didn't know who was right.

Mr Wakelin leaned his rifle against a tree. The others stopped and watched while he and I approached the trap. I reached into my pocket. Before we left the house, Mrs Wakelin had given me a left-over pancake wrapped in foil.

'What do you want to do?' Mr Wakelin asked me.

'Help me open the door, please,' I said.

One on each side of the trap, Mr Wakelin and I lifted the heavy door. Before it was even halfway up, a grey blur shot out between us and disappeared into the darkness.

The boy came out slowly, a few seconds after the mother wolf. He stopped in the mouth of the trap, blinking in the glare of the Jeep's headlights. He looked scared and confused.

'Here,' I said, handing him the pancake.

The boy sniffed the pancake, then stuffed it into his mouth and chewed ravenously. It was all gone in ten seconds. He licked the maple syrup off his fingers and looked to see if I had more.

I showed him my empty hands. 'All gone,' I said.

An eerie howl rose out of the forest about 50 metres away.

The boy peered into the darkness. *'Mwaa mwaa,'* he said.

I pointed at Mrs Wakelin, holding her two-year-old daughter. The boy had been about Tyler's age when he went missing. He must have known *some* English.

'Another *mwaa mwaa,'* I said slowly. 'Another family. They live just over that hill.' I made the shape of a hill with my hand, then did a walking motion with my other fingers to show someone climbing it. 'Go to them if you ever need anything.'

The boy seemed to understand. Stepping forward, he wrapped his arms around my waist in a brief, tight hug.

'*Daa daa*,' he said, smiling up at me.

Then he darted off into the forest to join his pack.

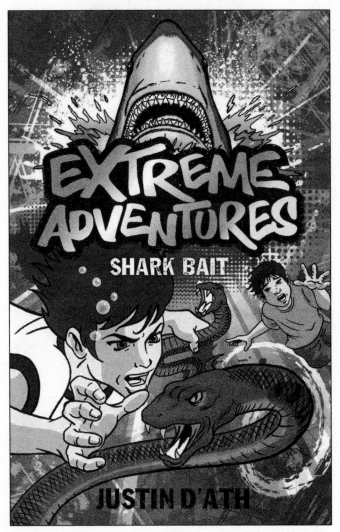

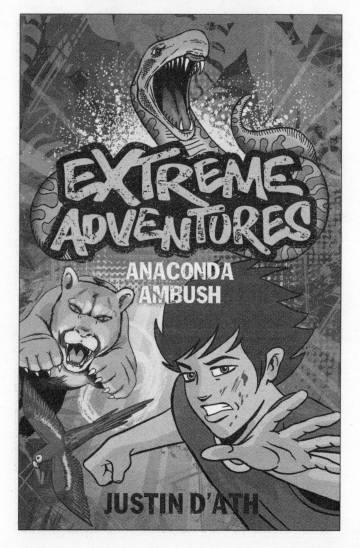

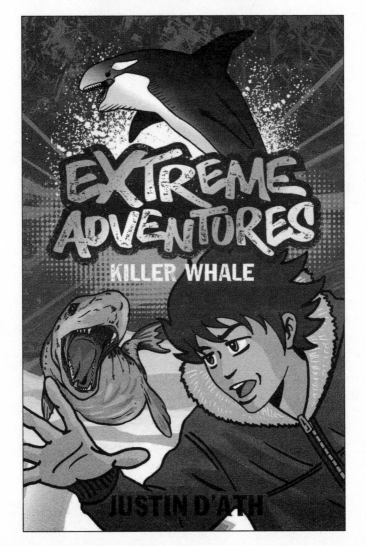